EAGLE DRUMS

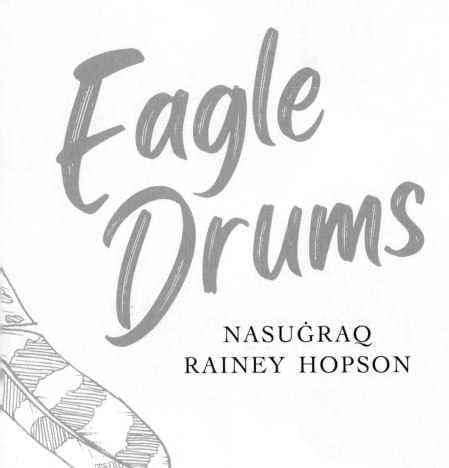

Eagle Drums

NASUĠRAQ
RAINEY HOPSON

ROARING BROOK PRESS
New York

Published by Roaring Brook Press
Roaring Brook Press is a division of Holtzbrinck Publishing Holdings Limited
Partnership
120 Broadway, New York, NY 10271 • mackids.com

Our books may be purchased in bulk for promotional, educational, or
business use. Please contact your local bookseller or the Macmillan Corporate
and Premium Sales Department at (800) 221-7945 ext. 5442 or by email at
MacmillanSpecialMarkets@macmillan.com.

Library of Congress Cataloging-in-Publication Data is available.

First edition, 2023
The illustrations were created using colored pencil, ink, and were edited in Adobe
Photoshop. The text was set in Garamond Premier Pro and Cochin. This book was
edited by Connie Hsu and designed by Aurora Parlagreco. The production was
supervised by John Nora, and the production editor was Mia Moran.
Printed in Canada by TC Transcontinental Printing

ISBN 978-1-250-75065-5
10 9 8 7 6 5 4 3 2

For Taktuk and Kanaaq, my Sunshine
Aaka loves you always and forever

CONTENTS

1

BROTHER

Sweat trickled down his back. He ignored it. A mosquito hummed in his ear; he ignored that, too. His body ached from being still so long; his feet were going numb again. Slowly, Piŋa flexed his toes to get the blood flowing. *A little longer*, he told his body, even though he had been waiting more than four hours already. His heavy-lidded eyes gazed straight ahead, focused on the movement of grass, the shifting of wind. His body moved only when the grass did, so slowly did he creep up on his prey.

The largest bull caribou gave a snort. With a sigh, the bull dropped down in the tall tundra grass, his ears twitching. Several other caribou took the bull's signal and settled down, relaxing their guard. Piŋa took note of which caribou were left standing, acting as sentinels for the herd, and crept forward again, slowly pulling his bow out and placing it in front of him. It had taken most of the day to get this close; he was determined not to let this chance slip away.

With a practiced movement, the boy nocked an arrow in his bow, pulled back, and released. It was timed, swift and sure, with the exhalation of the largest bull.

The arrow struck the bull with a soft *thump*. Quietly, as though falling into sleep, the great antlered head lowered itself to the tundra. The bull made no other sound and lay still.

Methodically, the boy shot the other resting caribou, one after the other, with the same silent, deadly accuracy. When the last sitting caribou died, it let out a soft mewling noise, alerting the herd. Nervously, the others hurried away.

The boy straightened from his crouch and stood, stretching his cramped muscles. He walked over to the largest bull and ran his hand slowly over the tips of the antlers. They were almost as tall as the boy. A quiet smile softened his face.

Carefully, the boy set the bull's head so it faced the boy's home to the west. He bent down and whispered in the bull's velvet ear, telling the bull how to find him. He opened the bull's still-warm mouth and placed a pinch of lichen on the tongue, then he took his sharpest obsidian knife and severed the third vertebra, releasing the bull's earthbound spirit to be born again. He did this for each of the fallen caribou. These small gifts ensured that he would be remembered as a kind and unashamed hunter, and next time their spirits would recognize him.

The boy had caught twelve caribou. His mother and father would be proud. When he had finished honoring their lives, he began the task of butchering.

With years of experience guiding his hands, his knife found all of the familiar spots to slice and cut and pry, and soon the animals were quartered expertly, wrapped in their own skins to keep the meat clean of tundra debris. Later he would bury the bundles in rocks to keep them cool and prevent animals from getting to them. He carefully examined the meat and the organs as he worked, using all of his senses to look for signs of disease that would make the animal unfit for eating. One animal showed signs of having been attacked by a bear recently, and a couple of the wounds were not healing right. He could see the sickness spreading from the wound into other parts of the animal. He set that one to

the side, making sure it did not touch the others. It would be fed to the dogs so it would not go to waste. The meat would not hurt the dogs, as their stomachs were much more robust.

The layer of fat on the largest bull's back was a finger length deep, showing how healthy and well-fed the animals were.

Piŋa could measure the season and age of the animal by the width of the fat and where it accumulated on the body. He could see how time manipulated the bodies of the caribou, like the length of daylight. Every animal was bound by these changes in their bodies as the moons turned and seasons passed.

That night, the boy lay down on his mat under the cooling light of a stubborn sun. Thoughts, like panicked ground squirrels, scurried through his mind. He ran his fingers lightly along his bow, watching how the smooth wood gleamed in the light, pearlescent with the years of use. It had belonged to his two brothers; each one had carried it before him.

His oldest brother, Atau, had crafted it by hand. The boy had heard stories of how it had taken years to find the perfect piece of wood, with the right height, heft, and suppleness. His brother had chosen well. The sinew had to be changed often, but the wood itself never discolored or cracked. When

Atau had disappeared long ago into the mountains, all that his parents found was his bow.

The middle brother, Maliġu, had then used it and carved images into its length. The carefully designed etchings depicted a love of the mountains, a reverence for hunting, and land animals in various poses. Behind each animal were carvings of the place and time of year the animals could be found. The entire bow was a map of sorts, teaching the boy all he needed to grow skilled in the taking of animals. Many of the etchings were almost worn away, but the boy knew its lessons by heart. Maliġu had also disappeared into the mountains, leaving behind only the bow and no clue to his fate.

The boy grimaced. He knew that his mother, seeing all the caribou, would be ecstatic at first, but he knew also that grief would wrap itself around her joy like fall-time darkness. Any excitement she felt would be forgotten as she began to tell stories about his missing brothers. She would talk about Atau's speed when quartering the caribou, his cuts clean and never hesitant, their skinned hides flawless and smooth, without any holes or thin areas. She would talk about Malġu's strength, how he could carry a full-grown bull caribou for at least a mile, and how he would work tirelessly for days without complaint. She would go on about the amazing hunters they had been and how proud she was of their prowess.

The boy would sit there and nod as he always did, letting her list all the wonderful attributes his brothers had had. And at the end of her speech, she would look at him, fear clouding her soot-colored eyes, wondering if he, too, would one day disappear. He loved his mother greatly and hoped one day he would only see his own reflection in her eyes, and not the shining memories of his brothers.

His father would say very little, of course. He would just pat the boy briefly on his back, a wide smile on his dark face, and whisper, "Good job, son."

At times, the boy thought his father took his brothers' disappearance the hardest. His silence became something you could almost see, a depth and heaviness in the air. He often sat alone, eyes scanning the distant horizon toward the mountains, one calloused and rough thumb gently following the surface of a carved ivory goose that Mother had made. There was nothing more fiercely protective than a goose defending its offspring. He'd kept the carving tucked into the inner lining of his parka ever since his two older children had disappeared. Piŋa didn't know what to make of his father's grief, so he focused on just being the best son he could be.

How can you compete with someone's memories, anyway?

A jaeger beat its wings in the wind, drawing the boy back to the present. The bird was headed for his carefully stashed meat. Annoyed with himself for letting his mind wander, the boy threw a stick in the bird's direction, letting it know that the meat belonged to another. When the bird had flown off, the boy rolled his body into tanned caribou hides and fell asleep to the sound of flapping wings and buzzing insects.

2

LEAVING

After making sure the meat was safely stored in temporary stone caches, he traveled home and grabbed the pack dogs, fashioned a travois from willow branches, and hauled all of his catch back with their help. Five days later, after two trips, the boy found himself examining a thin crack in the ice-covered wall of the sigluaq and wondering if he should shore up that part of the wall before the crack widened.

The sigluaq was built underground to preserve meat even when all the ice and snow had thawed above. Two feet beneath the earth lay a layer of ice that never melted, no matter the weather or season. The boy and his parents had

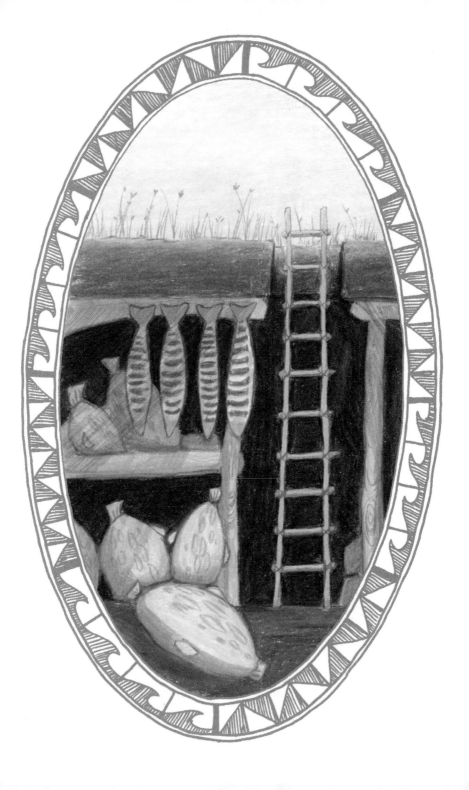

spent weeks chipping away at the frozen layer till it was large enough to hold the winter season's worth of food. Then they'd built a protective ceiling of wood and sod and whalebone above it. A ladder led up to an opening in the ceiling, which let in some light to see by. This storage mound was only a few years old, built to replace their previous storage space, which was much too large for just the three of them. It was still settling into the soil, so he was careful to inspect the walls whenever he was in there.

"You know, you should talk more, Piŋa," his mother said. To make room for the caribou, she was stacking frozen seal pokes, one atop the other, in the underground storage. "Your brothers knew how to tell a good story; how else are we supposed to know about your hunting?"

He ignored her and continued to examine the wall, hoping his silence would deter her from more conversation. Sometimes her need to fill the space with sound grated at him, like the droning of bothersome insects. He didn't want to talk about this. From the corner of his eye, he saw her brows draw down into a frown as she turned back to her task.

"If you told me about your hunting," she continued undeterred, "maybe I could sew a bag showing off your great fight. Wouldn't that be nice?"

In the semidarkness, the boy nodded in her direction. A long pause stretched out between them. He ran a finger over the crack and decided he wouldn't need to worry about it for a few seasons more, as it was still shallow.

"Well?" she said. "Aren't you going to say something?"

From her insistent tone, he knew he had to respond soon or he would be scolded.

He thought carefully about his mother's question. *Should I tell her the story of my numb feet? That would make an interesting bag design*, he thought. But instead he said, "They died well."

"Is that all you have to say?" She snorted softly, shaking her head. "Just like your father. Well, I can talk enough for the both of us, I guess. Hand me that other poke, would you?"

The boy and his mother maneuvered the already stored meat to make room for the fresh ones. They took care to make sure that the two did not touch—ocean on one side, land on the other, giving respect to both worlds. Soon enough, the underground larder was half-full.

Piŋa straightened and stretched the muscles between his shoulders as he finished distributing the allotted meat to his family's pack dogs. They were quiet as they worked on their portions of caribou, with only the occasional low warning growl for others not to get too close.

He took a deep breath, filling his lungs as he walked back to the sod house. The air carried the scent of plants turning in the fall-time weather, heavy with notes of water and fog and vague, fleeting promises of snow. The day was overcast with heavy clouds, typical of the shift from summer to fall. He changed the direction he was walking when he caught the smell of a cooking fire and the enticing smell of a meal. He made his way around to the entrance tunnel to his family's earthen home, to where the wind would be the least. The tunnel itself rose above the ground and was just shorter than he was.

His mother sat next to a small fire, and when she saw him, she waved him toward the shallow stone bowl that was perched on some coals. With the deft twist and turn of her hands, his mother tied her hair up in a quick braid and secured it with a slim ivory pick. She picked up her ulu, a wide, curved blade about the size of her palm, and drew it against a fine-grained rock a few times to sharpen its edge. The boy watched as she crossed her legs and silently began stretching and wetting the caribou skins to ready them for tanning. He smiled, realizing that the only time she was quiet was when she was concentrating on her skins. He crouched next to the fire and reached into the bowl for a piece of caribou meat. It steamed in the air, and hot fat dribbled down his sleeve. He took a bite; it was so soft and tender that it barely needed chewing, and it practically melted on his tongue.

From the direction of the beach, he could hear his father mumbling under his breath. He watched as his father worked in the distance, repairing a small tear on the skin of his kayak. His father hunted all that was of the ocean, and it showed in the darkness of his skin and the strength in his shoulders from days of paddling under the sun. He was the master of that domain—he knew the ocean better than any man before him. But he never chided the boy for loving the land instead of the sea, even though he'd lost two sons to it.

For eight turns of the moon, their hunting grounds were covered in snow and ice, which left only four brief, hectic cycles to gather as much food as they could for the coming winter. They'd always had food to last the long cold season and furs to protect them from the dangers of that season. His mother, a gifted seamstress, would make beautifully designed clothes, sewing hunting scenes into the hems of their parkas—ocean waves for his father and snowcapped mountains for the boy. Their kayaks were flawless, made of the strongest hides. Their sealskin and caribou-skin ropes never broke under pressure. Their knives maintained their finely honed edges, even after days of butchering.

In a land that could be dangerous and demanding, times were good for the boy and his family. They never took more than was needed, and they survived thanks to the animals and their kindness and generosity—and a heavy dose of luck. But the boy had no one else to compare his family to, for they rarely saw others, and when they did, they were cautious and kept their distance. The boy often wondered what those people thought when they saw his family. Did they want to take what his family had worked hard for? Were they planning how to push his family out of this rich territory? He remembered the camaraderie and the closeness he had had with his brothers, and he wondered what it would be like to get to know a stranger.

His parents rarely talked about how they had met. When they did mention it, it was always with carefully thought out words, as if they knew broaching the subject would stir up unanswered questions. He knew it was through a brief trade agreement between their fathers that ultimately had led to the two young people running away to be together, but Father refused to go into too much detail, instead waving his hands and commenting, "In this world, people have not found anything beyond being offended."

His mother looked up from her work, almost as if she heard his wondering thoughts. "We need more obsidian for knapping, son," she said quietly. "Your father is going to try for more fish down the coast before freeze-up. We can get one more batch dried and smoked and put into the siġluaq, so that means it will have to be you to go up into the mountains before it gets too cold."

"I will leave tomorrow," he replied. He took another bite of meat.

"You be careful," she said, a note of worry creeping into her voice. "And don't take longer than necessary."

Her words stung. Didn't she trust him yet? It had taken her two years to finally allow him to hike up to the mountains after his brothers disappeared. Despite her warnings that something up there would take him, just as it did his brothers, the boy had made many trips in the years since, and the only danger he had run into was a young male brown bear whose fur was now part of his parents' bedding.

Nothing is more dangerous than a bear, he thought, but

didn't dare say out loud. He turned away from his mother and dug back into the bowl for another piece of meat.

When the boy finished eating, he stretched out his tall frame on the ground next to his mother and watched the rhythmic movement of her hands as she scraped the dried membrane from the skin. Soon his eyes drooped, and he fell into a half slumber. In his mind, he went through the trip he would make the next day. He relaxed, belly full, as he considered what equipment to take and which route would be quickest. He would pack his waterproof socks made from seal intestines and leave behind the heavy throwing spears his father would probably push. He planned to move fast and did not want to get slowed by boggy tundra or unwieldy weapons. Eventually the soothing familiar sound of his mother scraping the skin lulled him into an afternoon nap.

Early the next morning, his mother hovered around him as he packed for his trip to the mountains, and he tried his best not to frown at her in annoyance. He tucked his elbows closer to his body as he moved around the tight space inside the sod house, stuffing supplies into his bag. His father watched from the sleeping platform, legs crossed as he absentmindedly rolled up a long length of braided sinew he was packing for his own trip down the coast in the opposite direction. His father's soft, deep voice rumbled under his mother's hovering movements.

"You can take two of my throwing spears, iġñiin, if you want. Over there." He gestured to the wall where a rack held their weapons. "Might help just in case. Better to have something rather than nothing when you need it." The boy raised his eyebrows at his father's suggestion. But he didn't reach for them, and instead grabbed an extra bowstring and stuffed it into his pack.

"It rained a few days ago. The lower trail might be wet. Maybe take the upper trail at the point," his father said. Again the boy raised his eyebrows in agreement while he slipped on his waterproof socks, making sure to tighten the straps of his caribou-skin boots so that they would not slip around when he walked.

I'm not a child anymore, he thought. *I know what I'm doing.*

His father glanced at his wife and sighed, then went back to wrapping the rope into a neat coil.

As soon as his pack was ready, the boy touched foreheads with his parents, ignoring the worry lines on their faces, and ducked down into the entrance tunnel.

The day was cool and breezy. Above him stretched a sky of the purest blue. The morning fog had quickly been burned away by the rising sun, and the intense red of the bearberry leaves on the ground competed with the bright yellow of the willow leaves. More than once as he walked, he startled fat lemmings gathering food. Their tiny, round rodent bodies erupted out of the grass and dashed ahead of him, whiskers twitching in annoyance, cheek pouches full, as they worked in a frenzy to get ready for winter.

After many hours of steady uneventful walking, the boy had almost reached the mountains proper. The slopes were jagged and stark against the sky, rising to block his view to the east. He could smell the sharp fragrance of ice and snow that rolled down from them, mixing with the warmer, earthy smell of the tundra. The calls of the sea-birds had long since disappeared, replaced by the chatter-ing of ground squirrels. Soon enough, the marshy tundra would be replaced completely by the dry brittle stones of the mountain slopes. He would reach the place of obsidian a little past midday. He had chosen the best route and was traveling fast.

Glad that the first half of his trip was almost complete, he decided to stop and eat. He found a small boulder to sit on, slipped his bow and arrows off his shoulders, and carefully unwrapped the paste that his mother had prepared for him. It was his favorite traveling food—berries and dried caribou meat suspended in whipped caribou fat. His mother had even added the leaves of a red flower that grew near their camp, a special tangy treat that made his mouth fill with saliva.

After eating and drinking a good measure of creek water from his water pouch, he closed his eyes and listened to the sounds of the nuna, listening to the world around him speak. To his left, a marmot whistled a warning. A heavy bumblebee vibrated above his head. The soft, sparkling sounds of tiny rocks tumbling down a nearby cliff drifted to him. As always, the sounds centered him. They quieted the echo of his parents' worries.

Suddenly, a golden eagle yipped, announcing itself. Its cry made the boy shiver with surprise as his eyes flew open wide. Golden eagles usually stayed farther inland, near more favorable hunting grounds. Excited, the boy searched the sky for the silhouette of the great bird, wondering if it would be close enough to catch. But the sky was empty. The boy kept scanning above him, sure that the eagle would soon appear.

Another series of cries rippled over the tundra; these

were much closer and came not from above the boy but from down low, in front of him. The boy turned toward the sound. The golden eagle hurtled toward him with alarming speed, a mere five feet above the ground, so close that the boy could see the slight adjustments it made midflight for the buffeting winds. The bird was huge, at least three times the boy's height from wing tip to wing tip. He had never seen a bird of this size. Its body gleamed gold in the sun, copper accents flashing at each feather tip. As it got closer, talons as long as the boy's forearm gleamed black in the sunlight and swung out in front of the great beast. Slowly the boy realized what the bird was doing. It was coming in for a kill, swift and dangerous—its eyes were focused on him.

3

SAVIK

The boy threw his body to the side. Too late, he realized that his bow and arrows were out of reach. He rolled again, pulling his obsidian knife from his belt. Dread flooded his mind like cold water, but with determination and resolve—and more than a little fear—he leapt up into a crouch, knife held low in front of him. He braced himself for impact, breathing harshly through his clenched teeth.

But nothing hit him. Instead, the air swirled around Piŋa, catching his hair and throwing bits of the dirt into his eyes.

He heard the sound of claws digging into stone, making his teeth itch. He turned his head toward where the noise was coming from. He saw the eagle had settled onto the boulder where he'd been sitting just moments before. The great bird scrutinized the boy, shifting its head side to side, holding its razor-sharp beak agape, wings pulled away from its body in readiness, muscles tense, body poised to launch.

The boy remained motionless, mind racing as he took stock of the situation, afraid to trigger the bird's attack instinct by moving. The world slowed down as Piŋa's heartbeat sped up.

A hundred thoughts poured through his mind.

The bird seemed winded from its flight, but it was large enough and quick enough to take him down without trouble. His light caribou-skin parka would offer no protection against talons made to rip and shred. There was nowhere to hide on the open tundra nearby, besides a few small and flimsy willow brushes. The knife he held would barely scratch the bird. He cursed himself for not carrying his father's heavy throwing spears.

His breath quickened. If the eagle attacked now, it would be a fight to the death. His instincts screamed to run, to put an object between them, or to surprise the bird and attack first. But he held his body as still as he could and slowed his breathing. His attention became razor sharp as he focused on every single movement the bird made.

The great bird cocked its head from one side to the other slowly, eyeing the boy with a predatory intensity. The pauses became longer between head swings, as though it was thinking about what it saw. After a few tense moments, the bird relaxed, lifted its head, and dropped its shoulders, tucking the great wings along its body. The beak closed with an audible slap.

The boy stayed crouched, waiting. Maybe the bird would judge him too much a fight, prey not worth the energy to take down. Maybe it would leave.

Maybe.

Finally, the eagle seemed to reach a decision. It stretched and flapped its wings once—which almost made the boy turn and run. Then the great bird began to shudder and shake its head.

Confused, the boy just stared. Soon the head shaking turned almost violent. Small feathers drifted to the ground as the bird tossed its head from side to side, and the topmost part of it began to peel away. The feathers receded as if being sloughed off, and with one final shake, the bird's face came down like a hood around its shoulders.

In front of Piŋa there now stood a man, clothed in a parka made of golden feathers tipped in shining copper. The man was at least two heads taller than the boy, with wide, heavily muscled shoulders. He had a clean-shaven, square-jawed face. Heavy brows framed dark-hooded eyes that dug into the boy.

For what seemed like hours, the two creatures—man and boy—stood facing each other. The boy was still crouched with the knife in front of him. The man, again shifting his head birdlike, examined him. Soon the muscles in Piŋa's legs began to cramp, but he ignored the pain and kept his eyes trained on the man's face, trying to read whether the man meant him harm. He had never had to read a stranger's face before.

I would have better luck reading a rock.

The boy knew what this creature was. Underneath his fear, stories crept up from Piŋa's memory. He heard his mother's voice speaking of animals while she sewed. "Animals are like us, Piŋa," she'd say, and she'd take a stitch. "They have all the same parts as us." Another stitch. "They choose to be animals, but when they need to be human, they take off their parkas. And then they are human for a while." Another stitch. "Respect them as you would any strong spirit, and never challenge them; you will always lose. Never disrespect any animal; they have long memories."

A being like this would never reveal themselves unless they had a purpose. Those who straddled the spiritual worlds did not interact with normal, everyday people like him.

All of this flashed through the boy's mind. *Respect*, his mother had said. Piŋa knew this being, if he chose to, could kill him quickly. Piŋa knew also that if he did not act soon, his body would be too stiff from staying still and crouched for so long to move effectively, no matter what his plans. Taking a chance that he knew might lead to his death, the boy made a decision. Slowly, he lowered the knife and set it on the ground in front of him. Then he offered up his empty hands to the man. His body tensed at the sudden vulnerability, and he forced his hands to unfurl. The sweat on his open palms began to dry in the cool autumn air immediately.

The piercing brown eyes watched his every movement, but the man gave no indication what he was thinking.

And what if I knew what he was thinking? How would that help me?

Piŋa took a deep, shaky breath, and for the first time in his life, he spoke before being addressed. "Elder," he said, making sure his tone was soft and as nonthreatening as he could muster. "I beg forgiveness for my show of weapons. I was surprised by your appearance." His voice cracked, but he straightened his shoulders, his eyes cast slightly downward so as not to make too much eye contact.

He glanced up to see the pupils in the man's eyes dilate with a predatory gleam. He quickly glanced away again.

Careful.

Swallowing the tightness in his throat, he spoke again. "Is there something you wish of me?"

The man began to laugh. It was deep and booming, filled with what sounded like genuine amusement. The laughter did little to relax Piŋa. The man tilted his head back; his teeth shone unnaturally white. Then he spoke. "Your brothers were not as smart as you, youngest one." His voice was confident and filled the space with its deep sound. "The oldest, the tall one with a mouth on him, he attacked me as soon as I landed." He shook his head. "Foolish." Amusement tinted the man's voice, but there was an undercurrent of disdain. "The rounder one, the one that froze and did not speak. He refused my request in the end. Also foolish."

The mention of his brothers made Piŋa's throat tighten, and he slowly lowered his hands to his sides. The grief he held for his brothers rose in his chest and gripped his heart, making this already surreal situation darker. He clenched his jaw at the flippant way the man described them.

Even more on edge, he waited for the man's next move.

"You may call me Savik, little boy."

And, indeed, the man reminded the boy of a knife, deadly and sharp.

"It is a name that will do, easy for your human mouth to pronounce," said Savik. And then, so swiftly that the boy did not see the movement, the eagle man was standing in front of him. His face was so near that the boy could smell his breath—and it smelled of blood.

"And as to what I wish of you, you will come with me now." He paused. "Or you can die like your brothers. Choose now."

Again, the way this man spoke about the end of his brothers' lives stung, clouding the level of fear he should have had. In that moment, the boy could think only of his parents. He knew that they would mourn him, as they mourned his brothers, if he did not return. The thought of their deep sadness made him speak up again. "What of my parents? How long will I be gone? Who will care for them and hunt the land?"

"Your parents will survive, as they did when they lost

their other sons. Come with me now, boy, or die. There are others who can take your place. Choose."

The boy knew his parents would want him to live, for he would probably be the last child they could have. He knew he would try his best to return to them, but to do that, he needed to stay alive. He also knew that he could not go unarmed. He gestured to the boulder behind Savik. "I will go with you, on the condition that I be allowed to take my bow."

Again the man laughed. "You may take your bow," he said. Savik reached over and took the bow in his right hand. "But I won't have you annoying me with arrows at my back." With one long black fingernail, he severed the bowstring. "Bring your gear, boy. We will be walking a long distance. Do not try to flee; I will find you easily." With that, he tossed the bow to Piŋa, turned, and with long, determined strides began walking toward the mountains.

The boy quickly gathered up his gear and followed the man, making sure not to leave anything behind for his parents to find. He hoped they would guess that he had met a different fate and that he would try to return.

4

NOISE

Savik and the boy traveled in silence. They pushed forward at a merciless pace. At first Piŋa fought the urge to break the quietude with talking, a feeling he was unused to. But by the fourth night, that need was overshadowed by the strangeness of his journey. The lack of talking allowed him to focus on what was happening around him and gave him some time to observe the being that took him.

Savik would only stop when it was obvious that the boy could not go on any longer. The boy was amazed at Savik's stamina; the man seemed never to need rest. Every once in a while, he would catch Savik popping his muscles and joints loudly with satisfied groans or scratching vigorously at his thick dark hair, as if his human form might be uncomfortable. At night Piŋa would roll himself in his thin caribou sleeping bag, but Savik would do his odd stretches and then fall asleep in a sitting position with no extra covering. He found himself wondering as he observed the man if Atau and Malġu had been smarter than he was and had brought Father's heavy spears. They were so much stronger than Piŋa, in more ways than one. They had been gone for so many seasons, and yet the pain of their loss was fresh in his mind. With effort he pushed the thoughts of his brothers away and tried his best to focus on his situation.

Pay attention.

With sudden dread, the boy remembered how winded Savik had been at the boulder. He realized then that they must be a great distance from Savik's home. Hoping to be able to guess how far they were from his own home, he would tie a knot in the cut sinew dangling from his bow for every full day they walked when they stopped to sleep. With every knot they traveled farther from his parents, the possibility of never seeing them again grew and grew like a stone in his gut.

After fourteen days of eerily silent traveling, during one of their brief rests, the boy mustered up enough courage to speak. "Elder Savik," he asked, "why did you take me?"

"We took you so that you can learn how to atuq, uamit, and niqinaqi," Savik replied.

Puzzled, the boy ventured to ask another question. "What do you mean, ah-tuuq, oo-ah-mitt, and nee-kee-naak-ki, Elder?" They were words he had never heard before, and he had to pronounce them carefully, rolling them around his mouth like tiny foreign pebbles.

But Savik did not answer. The man simply snorted in disgust and gestured for the boy to get up so they could continue traveling.

They traveled up into the mountains for over a turning of the moon, climbing ever higher. Loose shale, giant boulders, and sharp-edged stones replaced the deep tundra soil. When they could, the boy and Savik followed sheep trails in the high mountains, narrow pathways that wound up to the tops of the mountains in a haphazard zigzag of nooks and crannies and small dark caves.

Each night after the boy was settled, Savik would leave and return with game. Mostly it was a piece of sheep or caribou, sometimes fish or rabbit. The chunks of meat looked ripped apart, the edges rimmed with jagged marks. Piŋa chose not to think too much about how those marks were made.

Soon it was cold enough that the boy began to shiver whenever they stopped. When Savik noticed this, he brought back the skin of a small young brown bear, still damp and bruised with blood.

The boy mimicked his mother as best as he could remember, running his hands over the hide as he used his knife to scrape the raw side clean. He winced as he examined his work. He imagined his mother chiding him for doing such a bad job. Most of the time she would laugh and take over for him. In the end, the bearskin had a few small holes and some too-thin areas that might tear later, but it would do. Its warmth made his mother feel a tiny bit closer.

They had just arrived at a new camp for the night when Savik gruffly ordered the boy to stay and pointed to the hindquarters of a fat ram, enough food for a few days. Then he left.

The first night there Piŋa slept deeply, only waking once the hesitant sun touched his face. He got up and repacked his knife and water pouch and the tightly rolled bearskin. He sat and waited for Savik to come back and begin the journey again, his pack slung across his lap. When the sun dipped low on the horizon and the cold crept back into his parka, he made himself a small fire and cooked some more of the meat, piling stones around the fire so that they magnified the warmth. Still he waited. That night as he slept, he dreamed of dark claws raking across stone.

Once he realized he was going to be there alone for a while, he took the time to look over his gear and to gather what roots and plants he could, as the diet of nothing but meat was making his stomach cramp. He found some small withered ippiq roots, which were a bit dry but still edible, and some bright red kimmigñaq berries, which were sweetened a bit by the fall-time frost. He dug into his pack and found his beaver-tooth knapping tool and resharpened a couple of spots on his obsidian knife. He removed the cut string from his bow and prepped the new string he had brought so that he could easily slip it into place in a hurry. He didn't know if he would be needing his weapons soon. If he was going to be left alone for long periods of time in the future, then he might as well be prepared to fend for himself—or defend himself if he was going to be attacked again. The sounds of claws scraping against stone echoed from his dreams.

If I didn't have a chance then, then what chance do I have now?

But he couldn't just dismiss that path. *Better some than none*, his father would say.

On the third night as the sky darkened, he sat staring at the dying embers of his small fire and chewed the ippiq roots slowly, letting the saliva in his mouth rehydrate them. Tiny flames danced on the surface of the coals. They reminded him of his mother's oil lamp. Even on the darkest and coldest of nights during the winter, she would tend to those delicate flames, making sure the moss wicks always had oil to burn.

His mind and his heart wandered, filling the void around him. It was then that he heard the noise.

It resonated through his body, tickling the hairs on his arms and making them stand up. It was a slow, steady pulsation, begging him to move. Then the wind came back, drowning out the sound.

When it returned a few moments later, the boy realized that it wasn't a sound at all, but a deep rhythmic vibration that seemed to come from the mountains themselves. He could feel it in his jaw and his chest.

On the morning of the fifth day, Piŋa woke to the sounds of Savik moving the stones of the fire around as he tried to coax the embers back into flame. The mysterious sound dipped in and out around them, like waves on a shore. Savik gestured for the boy to get up and pack.

It was almost a week of traveling again before he gathered enough courage to ask about the sound. The subtle thumping vibrated through the stone and permeated the air around them. He could hear it clearly now, could feel it in his bones when he stood still. Carefully, he moved toward Savik, who also seemed to be listening.

"Elder Savik, may I ask you, what is that noise we are hearing? And why does it grow louder each day?"

The boy's voice startled the man. Savik pointed a black-taloned finger toward the top of the mountain, and his face softened a bit as his gaze ran up to its heights. "That, young boy, is my mother. The sound grows louder because we get nearer to her. We get nearer to my home."

And with that, he turned his face from the boy, and Piŋa knew not to ask any more questions. *What creature could make such sounds?* he thought.

Savik pushed him harder the closer they got to the mountaintop. Piŋa was exhausted, his legs leaden and sore. During their frequent breaks, the boy would gingerly pull his feet from his caribou-skin boots in order to examine them. Bits of his skin stuck to the inside of his boots, prompting fresh waves of pain. The bottoms and sides of his feet were peppered with angry blisters rubbed raw, blisters that got no relief from being aggravated by sharp mountain rocks through his thin-soled boots. He did his best to care for his feet, wiping them clean and drying them out in the cold mountain air. That same air caused his lips to crack and bleed, turning his exposed skin raw. He rubbed leftover bear fat from his bedding into them for relief, but the pain became worse as he grew weaker.

Water was scarcer as they got higher, so he looked for pockets of ice hidden in crevasses, tiny streams of snowmelt, or what he could catch when it rained. He had to stop to rest more often. It seemed as if there was never enough air for the boy to breathe, and his lungs burned and ached. Still Savik marched on.

The sound was so ever present now that the boy could not remember a time when it had not been there. He walked a few paces behind Savik, body bent underneath the weight of his pack. He kept his eyes on the back of the man's boots, doggedly following, wishing for an end to this mad journey.

At their last brief camp the night before, Piŋa had counted forty-six knots on his bowstring. It had been forty-six days, crossing a distance that was hard to imagine.

A giant mesa stretched before the boy. Tall stone walls at least twice the height of a grown man flanked the sides, forming a cup around the center. The stones buffered the wind, which was now mostly still. In the center, Piŋa saw five houses surrounding a large hill. Trails of blue smoke billowed from each house, and the faint smell of cooking made his stomach growl and cramp with hunger. Skins dried on racks, and various meats hung next to them, curing in the sun. It looked as if a large family had made this aerie their home. It was some time before the boy realized that the village seemed empty—not even a dog to announce their arrival.

Savik turned to the boy, and for the first time, Piŋa saw a smile on his lips. It was unsettling.

"First, you will meet my mother, boy. She has more words for you than I do." He turned and began walking to the center of the village. The boy stumbled after the eagle man, eyes wide as he tried to get a better look at his surroundings. The sod houses looked normal to him, except for the entrance tunnels, which were taller than the one built into his family's house.

And there was another odd detail. At his home there would be worn paths between the buildings and the other areas they frequented. Here there were no tracks between the buildings, only stretches of thick grass and wildflowers. He also noticed large, thick driftwood logs—some so wide that they came up to his knees—placed around the entrances of the sod houses. When he got close enough, he saw they were covered in deep gauges, as if from large claws. A shiver went down his spine.

They approached the large hill in the center, and when they turned a corner, he saw what looked like a long tunnel entrance. He realized then that the hill was hollow, a massive sod house. Larger than anything he had ever seen before. Easily twenty times the size of his own home. When they got to the entrance of the structure, he paused, pulled together what small scraps of courage he had left, and entered.

5

MOTHER

The smells hit him first. He recognized the heavy scent of burning oil lamps mixed with the deeper odor of people living in close quarters. A waft of tanned hide tickled his nose and brought memories of home to his mind. But one smell arose above all the others. It reminded Piŋa of a seagull he had once found lying dead on the beach—an odd combination of feathers and rot. He took this all in as he waited for his eyes to adjust to the dim light inside.

After a few moments, he began to make out shapes in the darkness. Two golden eagles flanked the great hall near the entrance, perched on thick driftwood logs. They were the color of wet tundra, a rich reddish brown. Both were darker than Savik in eagle form and slightly smaller, less bulky, but no less intimidating. Each trained an eye on the boy, silently observing every movement. *Guards of some sort*, Piŋa thought. Carefully, he dipped his head in their direction, but they did not move.

The hall was at least four times the height of a man, and the ceiling towered above him in a gentle arch. Thick pillars of driftwood and pale sun-bleached whalebone ran the length of the building, and several living and storage areas lined the sides. Lit seal-oil stone lamps were sporadically placed throughout, leaving most of the hall in darkness. He guessed that the eagles didn't need very much light to see.

Here and there he saw movement as shadowy human-like figures walked along the halls or sat working on projects. The sounds he heard were hushed and ghostly, a murmur of low voices and a strange whistling and chirping.

Savik shoved the boy forward, making him stumble. He turned around, and Savik pushed him again, waving him toward the back of the sod house, before ducking out the entrance, leaving the boy alone. Piŋa took slow steps toward the back of the sod house, where the darkness was deepest and barely visible lamplights twinkled in the far distance.

He felt eyes on him as he walked, and what quiet conversation he could hear quickly stopped as he approached them.

After a few more minutes of his slow, shambling shuffle, he reached the rear of the building. The back of the hall was walled off. A soft light emanated from a large opening, framed by wood heavily adorned with shallow carvings.

Gritting his teeth, he quickly stepped into the room, not wanting to delay his meeting with Savik's mother. The room was brighter than he expected, and he blinked away tears as he scanned his surroundings.

Then he saw her, sitting in a mound of skins piled high, like a throne. They gazed at each other, and in that moment, they both seemed unimpressed.

For one thing, she was old. Not just aging, but *old*. Her thin hair was silvery white, her dark skin lined with a myriad of wrinkles. Her jowls sagged, giving her an almost permanent frown. Her parka, though at one time it must have been magnificent, was soiled and tattered. In one gnarled hand, she held a twisted branch that she rubbed with her stained fingers. The smell of rotten meat rose from her, he thought, though he made sure that his face did not show his displeasure. He glanced at her eyes.

They were the color of the pyrite he sometimes found

on the beach, shimmering with gold and catching the light as they moved, youthful and sharp.

"You are disappointed in me, young one?" Her face wrinkled into different shapes. He thought she might be smiling. "I might say that I am also disappointed. You are young, and young ones often do not listen as they should. They think they know everything." Her voice, too, was young and invoked in him the memory of snowbirds calling in the springtime—sharp against his ear, high-pitched and clear in tone. Not the gravelly voice he expected from a woman her age.

Suddenly, Piŋa felt ashamed, though he did not know why. He tucked his chin to his chest and stared at the floor.

"But you will have to do for my purposes," she said. "I am running out of time." With that, she crooned deep in her throat, a noise only a bird would make.

The boy heard the rustle of feathers coming from behind him. His pulse raced, and his ears popped as his blood quickened.

She noticed his alarm. "You will stay with me. They have gone to gather the things you will need. My daughters will show you where you will sleep. Has the eldest told you why you are here?"

He frowned slightly, and then realized she was talking about Savik.

"Yes, Aana. He has told me I am to learn, Grandmother." His throat was dry, and his voice crackled across the space between them. He stared back at the floor in front of him, willing his heartbeat to slow down.

"And has he told you what will happen should you refuse?"

"Yes, Aana, I will . . . join . . . my brothers." The rustle of hides caught his attention, and he glanced up to see her leaning forward, the tip of her branch pointed at him.

"And do you wish us harm for what we have done to your family? Do you hold that as your brothers did?"

He took a deep breath through his mouth to avoid gagging from her stench and thought her question over, searching for the truth in his feelings. Revenge would not bring back his brothers. Revenge would not give his parents their youngest son back. All he wanted was to return to his parents, no matter what the future held. *I just want to make it home.*

"No, Aana," he finally said. "I only wish to see my parents again, to hunt for them as a son would."

She leaned back into her skins and placed the branch

on her lap, sharp fingers rubbing the twisted curves. She squinted at him. "I believe you, boy. But you must never cross me or my children. You will eat and sleep tonight. Tomorrow, I will begin teaching you, and we will see if my opinion of you changes, or yours of me, ami? You will be here until you learn everything, so it is up to you how long you will enjoy our company."

She pursed her lips and looked him over carefully. "And what shall I call you? What is your name, boy?" He blinked in surprise at her question, only then realizing that Savik had never asked him his name, and cleared his throat before answering.

"Piŋasut is my name, but my family calls me Piŋa, Aana." She grunted; her golden eyes blinked.

"Your parents named you 'Three'? How interesting. Were your brothers named Atausiq and Maliġuk? One and Two, then?" He nodded. She snorted, and without another word, she curled up into her skins, piling them high until she vanished. Almost immediately, the mound of furs began to snore softly.

As he left the Eagle Mother's room, two women emerged from the dim light of the hall, one carrying a pile of furs, the other carrying a platter stacked high with steaming meat.

Their faces were long and pointed, and they shared their mother's golden eyes. They said nothing and gestured toward a corner of the house, right outside Eagle Mother's room, and laid the furs and platter on the ground. A short driftwood wall afforded him some privacy from the rest of the hall, and he leaned his pack and bow against it.

He walked to the platter, his stomach rumbling. The boy was surprised to discover the platter held boiled seal meat. The ocean was miles and miles from where they were, and the meat seemed fresh. The meat was soft, perfectly cooked, and cut into bite-size pieces, just like his mother would make it. After eating his fill, he crawled into the pile of furs, not even bothering to unroll them, and closed his eyes.

He thought of his family. He thought of his brothers. How brave they were in their final moments. Did it mean he was brave as well, or was he a coward to find himself here? Should he have fought more? Exhaustion finally shut down his wandering mind. He fell asleep quickly.

6

SONG

He awoke to a constant stabbing pain in his back. Instinctively, Piŋa leapt to his feet, reaching for his knife. When his vision cleared, he found himself staring into the golden eyes of the old woman, her body quaking with stifled laughter. Her overpowering smell flooded his nostrils and made him flinch. She held her stick in front of her like a knife and waved it in his direction.

"Shall we fight first, young one? Who do you think would win?" She laughed out loud, her voice echoing through the hall.

He sheathed his knife and averted his gaze. "I am not used to being awakened in such a way, Aana. Forgive my reaction."

"Hmm, there is that politeness again, boy. Come. We are ready to begin your lessons." She turned away and strode to the middle of the hall.

He was surprised by her quick movements and tall height. Even while hunched over, she was quite a bit taller than him. Her hands and face were the only skin showing, and he noticed that on top of her wrinkles, she also had fine downy pale hairs all over her skin that reflected the light and made her look like she glowed. Her long white, greasy hair was pulled back from her face and woven into thin braids that bounced with each of her steps. The beads that hung at the end of the braids hit each other as she walked, clinking softly.

In the center of the hall sat Savik and the two daughters. The daughters glanced briefly at him as he arrived. Though they looked similar, one was a bit older than the other, with fine lines at her eyes and around her frowning mouth. Her skin was darker, the type of shade from being outside for long periods of time. An isiġnaq-handled ulu hung from her belt; the green-colored stone glowed in the dim light, half-sheathed in leather.

The other woman was slimmer and wore a shorter parka with dark bird-feather leggings underneath. When she moved, the boy could see that the feathers were mostly white at the base.

His eyes turned to Savik, who held a wide, thin disc made of pale, almost translucent skin that was stretched across a wooden frame, with a small handle on one end. The large disc was about an arm's length across. In his other hand, Savik held a long, thin stick.

Was he looking at a weapon? A tool? *And what if it's a weapon? What then?*

The old woman seated herself next to Savik. She cleared her throat impatiently and pointed at the ground across from her.

"Sit!" she commanded. "We are not planning to harm you! Sit!"

Piŋa quickly sat down, his spine rigid with tension, and waited for the next command. But none came. Their staring made him nervous. He began to sweat.

"Now place your hand on your chest," the old woman said, "and tell me what you feel."

Confused, the boy stared wide-eyed at the old woman.

"What is the matter? Place your hand on your chest and tell me what you feel! Are you daft?" She turned and made a noise, a guttural trill in the back of her throat. She twisted her head and whispered to the younger daughter. She turned back to the boy with a stony look. "You may call this daughter Nautchiaq, for she brings light to my life like a flower. She will show you what we ask."

Nautchiaq gracefully stood up and leaned toward the boy, extending a slim hand. She smiled a little as she came close to him, revealing deep dimples on either side of her small mouth.

He closed his eyes, afraid of what might happen next. He didn't know what actions would be offensive to them, didn't know what mysterious lines were crossed that ended his brothers' lives. *Try not to die, try not to die*, he said to himself.

She wrapped her cold fingers around his and placed his palm flat on his heaving chest. She pressed it there firmly and then let go.

"Open your eyes, boy," the old woman said to him. "You look foolish."

Cautiously, he opened one eye and then the other.

"Now," the old woman said, "tell me what you feel with your hand."

They all stared at him expectantly.

He glanced down at his hand on his chest and frowned.

What mad thing is this? he thought. "I feel the skin of my clothes, Aana. And the bone of my ribs."

The old woman snorted and stabbed the air between them with the twisted branch. "Beneath the bone, boy. What do you feel beneath your chest bones?"

Concentrating, Piŋa pressed his fingers harder into his chest. Again he felt bone. The only other thing he could feel was . . . "My heartbeat, Aana. I feel the pumping of my blood."

"Show me what it sounds like," she said excitedly. "Beat your fist on the floor. Show me what the sound is." She leaned back, her face expectant.

Slowly, quietly, the boy thumped his fist on the floor, trying to mimic the double beat. But the sound was irregular, not like the steady beat of his heart. His face warmed in embarrassment as he glanced up to see all of them watching his movements. He stopped and sat still, brows drawn down as he glanced at the ground in frustration. He was a skilled hunter with bow and arrow and spear, yet why couldn't he do such a simple thing?

Nautchiaq sighed and returned to her mother's side. The Eagle Mother's face wrinkled into a look of exasperation.

"Uva." Savik grunted, getting his attention, and nodded to his own fist, which he thumped against the floor. *THUMP thump, THUMP thump.* The boy nodded and tried again. One was louder, he thought, so he struck the floor harder. The other was softer and came closer on the first. He struggled for a while, but, gradually, his fist began to beat in perfect rhythm with the pulse in his body. He relaxed into the oddly soothing sound.

Piŋa was so focused that at first, he did not notice the other sounds rising around him. Savik had begun to strike the edge of the large disc with the stick, softly, almost imperceptibly at first. Savik's beating, like the boy's fist, was perfectly timed with his heartbeat. The two sisters began to speak, but in a way that was unfamiliar to the boy. Their voices rose and fell in time with the pounding. As the combined sounds grew louder, the boy stopped and simply watched and listened, transfixed. Savik struck his instrument harder, filling the space with sounds that he could feel on his skin. The women stretched their necks toward the roof, pouring their golden words into the air. The Eagle Mother sat and stared at the boy, head tilted, golden eyes searching his face.

Soon the boy was able to make out the words:

His arrows
    were quick
Aa ya yai ai yaa
They welcomed
    death
Aa ya yai ai yaa
They loved
    him still
Aa ya yai ai yaa
Their brother
Aa ya yai ai yaa

They will
    come back
They promised
And give
    themselves again
They will
    come back
And go around
    the bend

For he is

    still loved by them

For his hand

    is kind

For he is

    still loved by them

Abruptly the sounds stopped. Savik carefully set down the round instrument. They stared at the boy expectantly. Breathing quickly, Piŋa stared into Eagle Mother's eyes. His arms were covered in goose bumps, and his throat was wrapped around emotions he couldn't quite name. The muscles in his chest felt tight, and his eyes watered. Eagle Mother smiled. She seemed pleased.

The sister's performance had brought back the day he had hunted the great bull tuttu in the tundra grass, the careful way he had treated their dead bodies, the words he had whispered in their velvet ears. Somehow through the eagles' performance, Piŋa had lived it from the *other* side.

A good hunter did not take a life lightly. He accepted his role as life-taker, not with regret or shame or fear, but with reverence. All hunters dealt with this in different ways, different rituals to ease the spirit of the animal, to connect

the hunter with his prey. *We are the eaters of souls: plant and animal. Living consuming the living.*

For those few moments, Piŋa had been tuttu. Caribou. He had felt the lichen in his mouth. Had felt how the caribou knew that he was there in the tall grass, had felt their submission and their judgment of his worthiness. He had felt their emotions, the fear, the many deaths they gave to him. The promise. The cycle of the relationship between hunter and hunted.

"What is this magic called, Aana?" he asked.

She leaned closer to him, eyes glittering as she nodded. She spoke softly. "It is not magic, boy, it is what every living thing contains. You are here so we can show you how it is done, so you can show others how it is done. Atuqtuni nakuuruq—it is good to sing. This is called *song*."

The boy nodded, determined, and he lifted his head to speak. "I am willing to learn, Aana. And I am a good listener."

At his words, the eagles smiled.

7

BEGINNINGS

The next morning, he awoke again to the Eagle Mother's prodding stick and to another lesson with the eagle family. They chose a different song for him to start with, a song about a hunter in a kayak getting lost in a fall-time fog on the ocean, paddling for days, wandering aimlessly in the nothingness. When he finally finds land, his immense joy is tempered by the fact that he does not recognize the place. As the fog lifts, he mourns feeling disconnected from his family.

It was a feeling Piŋa could identify with.

Aana's daughters taught him the words, making him repeat them over and over until he could recite it back word for word. Then they taught him how to sing the words while Savik drummed, how to mold the words around the beat and to pace them with the rhythm. Singing loudly over the beat of the drum, his voice was hoarse at first but eventually became strong and clear.

That evening, Nautchiaq brought his meal to his sleeping area, boiled caribou meat piled on a platter. As she set it down in front of him, Piŋa immediately knew that the meat was off. The musky odor of a caribou in rut stung his nose. When he turned to complain to Nautchiaq, she had already left. Resigned to this meal, he gingerly cut a small portion of meat and placed it on his tongue, closing his eyes as he forced a swallow. The animal musk clung to his throat as it went down. He couldn't finish more than a few bites.

He thought back to the caribou he harvested for his family, remembering the thickness of the fat as the caribou prepared themselves for winter. This meat they had given him had no fat at all, as the animal had burned through its stores fighting other caribou bulls during mating season.

Has it been that long already? At least two turnings of the moon?

The next day, he braced himself to speak up as they fed him again. This time it was Savik holding another equally strong-smelling platter of caribou meat. Piŋa blurted out his words before the eagle man could set down the meat on the floor.

"I can't eat that meat."

The man turned, his dark brows drawn down into a scowl. "What? Why not? It is fresh meat."

The boy grimaced as he gestured to the meat again. "The caribou has gone into rut; its meat is too strong-smelling for my stomach. It also doesn't have fat, which will make me sick eventually." He paused, trying to find a way to explain what he thought everyone would know.

Well, what humans *would know.*

He stumbled on when Savik answered with a more intensive scowl. "My stomach is not like . . . yours . . . I can't eat too much of this meat, and I have different needs. I need plants, fruit, roots, and hopefully some fat. Eating nothing but meat will make me sick." He continued in a rush. Savik looked down at the platter of meat and back up at the boy as he took in what Piŋa said.

"The fat we can find for you, but are all . . . plants . . . edible? Will *any* do?" Savik asked. His lip curled a bit when he said the word *plants*, as if simply the thought of ingesting them was unpleasant.

"No, some would make me ill, and some have to be picked at a certain time." Piŋa thought about the permanent frost that didn't disappear, now coating the low grass and scrawny, windblown brush that was clinging to the ground. A new knot of anxiety tied itself in his chest. He had never found himself without his family's stores of food for the winter. He searched his memory for stories his parents had told him about when they were young, during the lean years.

"There might be some found under the snow. At least enough to keep me healthy for the winter."

Savik sighed and scratched at his cheek, eyes looking in the direction of his mother's quarters.

"Fine. You can spend as much time as you need around our home to look for your . . . plants. We will figure something out if you need more than that." The man sniffed at the platter in his hands before leaving with it from the room. That day the boy went hungry.

The next morning, Savik showed up early to his room, holding two bundles, one larger than the other. The biggest one was half of a caribou, which the man effortlessly swung off his shoulders toward the ground. Piŋa braced himself for the strong smell of a caribou in rut but instead was met with the clean, familiar scent of fresh meat. Savik set it down, making sure that the skin protected the meat from any dust on the floor. The other bundle turned out to be several fish the length of his arm, grayling from the looks of it, frozen completely solid together into a single lump. Savik nodded at the meat.

"Do either of these have the fat you need?"

Piŋa crouched down and examined the caribou first. It was female, which was why there was no strong smell. He took his knife and quickly made a cut, looking for the white fat underneath the skin. There was a little there, enough to make a bit of his anxiety knot loosen. He scraped the ice off of one of the fish and was surprised to see the fish was round and well-fed, insulated in a layer of fat.

"Yes," Piŋa said, letting the relief show in his voice.

"We know a lake where the water doesn't freeze all winter. Easy to fish there," Savik said as he noticed Piŋa turning the fish over in his hands.

"Can I have a small oil lamp? To preserve some of the food? It would help me dry the meat and plants quicker."

Savik nodded and left the boy. Piŋa's shoulders relaxed as he worked on the meat and fish, briefly enjoying doing something so familiar.

Most of his days were filled with singing practice, but two or three times a moon he was allowed to wander around the eagles' aerie. He was happy to find that there was a good amount of plants to pick and use, though he could tell the lemmings had been harvesting from this same area. Several sturdy wooden racks were sprinkled among the houses, and hanging from them he could see items he recognized, like caribou skin and clothing set out to dry. Though there were also some items that he could not recognize at all. He stayed clear of the eagles' things as he walked along the sod houses. Piŋa looked forward to these days, even though winter had fully taken over and the bitter cold stung any exposed skin.

He pulled on mittens, which he made himself from caribou hides he saved, and used the broken tip of a caribou antler to dig down through the snow, searching for winter-preserved plants underneath. He discovered more frozen kimmigñaq berries, their bright red juice staining the snow pink, making them easy enough to find, and some ippiq roots that he carefully and slowly extracted from the solid ground. He even found some tilaaqiaq plants that he used to make a strongly fragrant drink that warmed him and gave him energy. He carefully dried what he could to make them stretch out for the months ahead.

Better some than none, he heard his father's rumbling voice in his head.

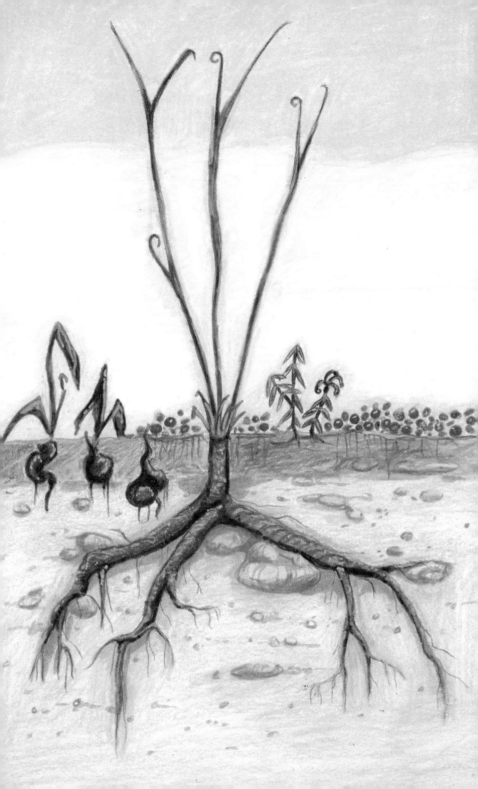

8

MEMORIES

Another turn of the moon passed. The winter sun hid longer and longer beneath the mountains as Piŋa learned as quickly as he could.

Eagle Mother, Savik, and Nautchiaq were the only ones who spoke directly to him. He never learned the older daughter's name, but he had taken to calling her Isiġnaq because of her ulu. The ulu had a flawless nephrite jade handle that glowed a bit when the light hit it right. She never corrected him or said much. Nautchiaq was chattier, but she was often quieted by a look from her mother. In fact, no one really spoke to him at length besides the Eagle Mother and Savik. The others in the sod house quickly scurried away if he approached them. At first, Piŋa thought it was because he was a stranger, but as time passed, he realized this was deliberate. He brought it up to the Eagle Mother one day as they took the short walk from the place they slept to the center of the hall. Her eyes squinted sideways at him, and she stabbed at his arm with her twisted stick, making him wince.

"And what would you do if you knew the others? What would you do with this information, boy?" She stopped walking and waited for his answer. Piŋa felt that this was a test and was afraid to give the wrong answer.

"Maybe get to know them?" he said. "I don't know."

"We are not humans, boy. We are . . . more. And personal knowledge of us can give you power over us. So, we are better to be careful, ami? What would happen if you knew our favorite food? Our favorite song? Our names to call us whenever you felt like it? What soothes us or indebts us? What then? What would you do with such knowledge?"

The boy looked down at his boots, thinking about these questions. The Eagle Mother waited for his response.

"Then why do you talk to me, Aana? Aren't you afraid I will have influence over you?" he asked instead of answering her question. A wide smile crinkled her face, showing what few stained teeth that she had left. She lifted the crooked stick so that he could see the length of it. He had never had the opportunity to examine it closely before. He noticed that the shape of the stick, with its curves and bends, was not natural like he had assumed. It had been carved from a single piece of wood. He could make out what looked to be sinew of different thicknesses and delicate thin strips of leather in a multitude of colors embedded into the wood. The unassuming stick was decorated from tip to tip.

"This is where I keep my memories—or specifically, one type of memory. This reminds me of all of those humans in the past who dared to use something against me. To try and control me. A record of their methods and what tactics they used." Piŋa's eyes widened as he realized what that meant, that these were people that the Eagle Mother had defeated. She smiled even wider, exposing her bluish tongue. "I am old, and there were many humans that I had known before you, and I will probably know many after you. Would you like to be a string on my stick? Hmm?"

The boy froze in his tracks. Eagle Mother chuckled low in her throat and turned down the hall to her waiting brood.

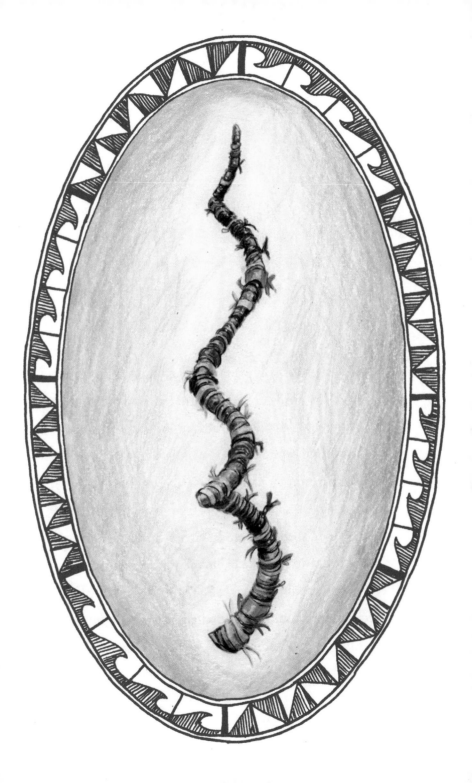

9

QIIAUN

Soon the fresh caribou and sheep meat disappeared from his meals. Piŋa knew that during the coldest part of the year, the herds split up into smaller groups and were almost impossible to find in the vast mountains. What animals were left were lean from running from the wolves. The eagles instead brought him piles of Arctic hares, their meat leaving a bitter taste in his mouth from their diet of willow bark. He took care to keep what he could of their fur pelts and eventually fashioned himself a tunic to wear when he went foraging for plants in the increasing cold. They continued to bring him fat fish, and once even brought a small seal. The fat from the seal would save him that winter, providing both oil for his lamp and fat to keep himself from starving. The sealskin he used to make a pair of waterproof boots that replaced his worn set.

Winter moved in with vigor, sharpening the air so that it hurt his lungs and forced him to breathe shallow through his mouth. His body became as lean as a hare from the sparse diet.

One morning, Savik came in place of Eagle Mother to get Piŋa for his daily lessons. They walked the few minutes to the center of the hall in silence and arrived to find stacks of dried skins, wood, and a haphazard array of tools. Savik found a spot to sit. The boy carefully sat across from him, eyes wide at the change in routine.

Savik cracked his knuckles one by one, glaring at the boy. The silence stretched between them like an uncrossable valley. Though Piŋa had gotten used to the eagle man's intimidating presence, the boy was always afraid that he would do something to make Savik kill him like he did his brothers. He was continually locked between trusting these creatures—*not humans*, Aana had said—and feeling like he was not safe with them and may never be safe again.

Savik pointed to the floor next to him, where a caribou

skin had been placed. The boy got up hurriedly and sat beside the eagle man, clasping his hands in his lap.

Once he was settled, Savik picked up the round, flat instrument in front of him, gripping the short handle at the end loosely. He gestured at the instrument.

"Qiḷaun, drum." He handed it to the boy. Piŋa gingerly took the instrument—the drum—by the handle. He was surprised by its weight and uneven balance, and he quickly adjusted his grip. The handle was carved from walrus ivory and was attached to an almost perfect circle of thin wood. A thin skin was lashed tight across it. He ran a hand over the skin, and it hummed as the calluses on his finger caught on the surface and amplified the sound.

"Ka-lawn." The boy rolled the word around in his mouth.

"No, boy. It's KEE-laun." Savik corrected him, pointing to his throat at the guttural first sound of the word.

"Qiḷaun," Piŋa repeated.

Savik nodded and took the drum from the boy, gently setting it to the side. He reached behind him and pulled out a long, thin strip of light-colored wood and placed the piece into Piŋa's lap. The boy picked up the wood to examine it as Savik spoke.

"We will start with the wood. Wood doesn't want to

curve. It grows as straight as possible, reaching for the sun. So, to get it to curve, you have to be patient and gentle, take your time, coax it with heat and water. You can measure a man's patience by the roundness of his drum." His lips curled a little into a half smile at his own cleverness. The boy was surprised by the ... joke? *Do eagles have a sense of humor?*

Savik continued. "You will watch me a few times, then try yourself."

The boy was already somewhat familiar with the intricacies of woodworking, and found the process to be similar to making snowshoes, though much more complex, as he spent the next few days making the drum. Savik was a strict teacher, demanding perfection and understanding at every step. He made the boy repeat each step countless times, often grabbing the drum from Piŋa's hands, undoing all the work, and forcing him start over.

Each time he did this, it grated at the boy's already raw nerves. Savik seemed to revel in the boy's frustration. Piŋa was used to this method of learning—he learned everything from his brothers by following their example, taking their knocks and teasing in stride—but at home with his family, there had been warmth and breaks and encouragement from his mother and father. He got none of that here. Even the two eagle sisters, though nothing close to gentle, had at least more patience than Savik did. When the boy hesitated or took too long to do his bidding, Savik would walk off in frustration, sometimes leaving him alone for the whole day.

A qiḷaun was made to be somewhat flexible. Nothing was rigid or solidly fixed, and all of it was held together by braided sinew, which flexed and shrank and stiffened over time as it aged. The hide that stretched across the drum was so thin that he could see the shape of his own hand through the open mouth of the drum. Savik told him it was made from the lining of internal organs from animals—or in some cases the delicate back skin from young caribou or sheep—and the surface was marked with faint veins, making each drum wholly unique. While Piŋa worked, Savik sat to the side and tended to the finished drums, often rubbing oil or water in the skins, keeping them moist and supple so that the sound was true and the skin would not split. Sometimes Savik replaced old sinew with new, or tightened loosening knots. In many ways, the drum was alive, reacting to the world around it like a living creature. Each one hummed with a different note and tone when struck, each with a different voice.

After one turn of the moon, their corner of the great

hall was filled with drums in various stages of being built, alongside a large pile of ruined materials from the boy's mistakes that they would find some use for later.

Savik had insisted that the boy learn to make different sizes of drums. Piŋa could now work with a variety of materials and skin, ensuring that no matter the hunting season, he would always find a way to make the drum.

One morning, Savik stood over the boy's shoulder as Piŋa attempted to tighten thick sinew around a drum, lashing the skin down tight across the circle of wood. This part of the process was always tricky and required just as much luck as skill. This drum was the largest Piŋa had tried making; it was unwieldy and awkward, and the sinew was uncooperative, even with the special self-tightening knot he was using. The boy's face grimaced. Sweat dotted the bridge of his nose.

"Your knot isn't right," said Savik.

"It's fine," the boy said in a tight voice.

"Your knot isn't right. Take it apart and do it over."

The boy glared at the man briefly, then set the drum down. The sinew knot loosened as soon as he released it, and the oiled sheepskin slid from the wooden frame onto the ground in a messy, unappealing lump. From the corner of his eye, he could see Savik clench his jaw, skin darkening with the insult. Piŋa held his breath, waiting to see what his reaction would be. Savik grunted at the boy's obvious disrespect, waved an angry hand in his direction, and walked off, his heavy steps pounding out his displeasure. The boy exhaled in relief.

Savik would come back tomorrow; he always did. Often in a sourer mood than usual.

Piŋa stared at the unfinished drum in front of him, his mouth pursed with annoyance and anger. He reached over and pulled at the damp sinew till it came loose from the drum.

"The knot is fine," he whispered at the dark empty space around him.

10

PTARMIGAN

It had been a while since the eagles brought him any meat at all, a couple of weeks at least. Everyone living in the aerie waited for winter to break its grip on the world. The skies were filled with storm after winter storm as the seasons fought with each other and made it impossible for the eagles to fly and hunt. Piŋa was happy he had a small amount of food preserved and hidden away for times like these.

Then one day the skies cleared long enough for a bit of hunting and gathering. Piŋa pulled on as many layers as he could and ventured out to scour the ground under the snow for any plants or berries he could find. After a few hours, his face had gone numb and he could barely move his fingers. He made his way back to the hall empty-handed.

When he reached his sleeping area, he was surprised to see six rock ptarmigan hanging from a hook that he used for his winter gear. Seemed the eagles had better luck than he had. Piŋa quickly shed his gear and began to dress the birds for cooking. He was excited for the change in diet, knowing that late-winter ptarmigan hadn't started eating willow buds yet, so their bellies would be full of berries and other edible herbs, and their meat would be sweet and tender without the taste of bitter willow.

As he worked on the ptarmigan, carefully plucking their snow-white feathers and setting them aside to use later, the smell of the birds on his hands tickled a memory as gently as the tiny downy feathers tickled his nose.

Wintertime was always his most favorite season when he was young. Late spring was usually hectic with cleaning out the siġluaq and preparing for the hunting seasons. Summer was filled with travel to escape the hordes of mosquitoes, and fall was the busiest, as they hunted and gathered in a frenzy to fill their stores for the coldest parts of the year.

During most of the year, Piŋa's older brothers went away on hunting trips or on supply runs. But in winter the family spent time together indoors, enjoying their hard-won meals and telling stories and jokes by lamplight while they repaired and replaced gear. Even after all these years, he could still hear Atau's loud, barking laugh and Malġu's rumbling chuckle echoing through their family's sod house.

His earliest memory of them all together was the day they taught him to make ptarmigan snares. He was about five years old, finally tall enough to travel the deep snow, but still too young to go far from their home.

The long winter was giving way to an early spring, and soon his brothers would be off to scout the trail for his family's seasonal migration to their summer camping grounds. The deep snow glittered in the sunlight as the top layer melted and refroze at night. Atau led the way, using his towering height to aim their small party like an arrow through the dense, leafless brush. He took long steps in the deep snow, using his forearms to clear the willows, all while mumbling colorful curses at the snow clinging to his boots. Malġu walked closely behind Atau, using his girth and weight to break through the snow so that Piŋa could follow in his wide footsteps. As Malġu waded, he pointed here and there at the willows and their fuzzy little buds that had appeared in the early spring sun. The air smelled green and new, like melting ice and fresh dirt.

They came to a clearing where the snow was peppered with tiny shallow tracks that barely broke the surface, a million little Y-shaped impressions, each barely a finger long. Piŋa looked into the willows, expecting to see the animals that made all of these tracks, but the willows were empty. The animals were long gone because of all the noise the boys had made as they approached.

Atau reached up and began snapping the tops of the willows, careful to keep the buds intact till he had gathered an impressive armful. Malġu sat and pulled out some braided sinew lengths and motioned for the boy to come forward. Piŋa sat in front of him, eyes wide as he watched Malġu's nimble fingers create a sliding loop with a special knot. It was like a lasso with a short tail.

"Piŋa, watch closely. Watch how I make the knot." He repeated the knot over and over in slow motion with several lengths of braided sinew, making sure that the boy could see how it was done. "Now you try," he said.

The boy took his hands out of his mittens and practiced tying the special sliding knot while Malġu watched, pausing only once in a while to rub his hands together to warm them. A couple times Malġu reached over and undid the boy's work completely with a gentle rumbling. "Almost, almost. Good job, baby brother. Good job." But soon they had a pile of about ten small loops, each one about a man's handspan across.

When Piŋa finished, Atau began creating a wall about as high as his knee in the clearing using the willow branches he had broken off. He stuck the branches in the snow so that the springtime buds were at the top. They all crouched around one of the gaps in the short willow-branch wall.

"Ptarmigan are not fancy or smart, which is why there are so many. If you're not smart, then you have to be plentiful!" Atau said, and then laughed his loud barking laugh. Malġu's round belly jiggled a little with quieter chuckles. "Come, baby brother, and let me show you how to do some population control—and get some tasty springtime birds for mother's stew." They wove the sinew loops between the willow-tip buds they had stuck in the snow, carefully constructing a short wall.

"See here, ptarmigan behave the same always and forever. They fly and walk along willows searching for the buds at the tips to eat. They *love* them some early springtime willow

tips, ami? But they can be lazy. If they see or smell them on the ground, they will eat those first." Atau made his fingers do a happy little dance as he walked his hand along the wall, smacking his lips as he made his hand pretend to eat the buds. "And when the silly birds walk through the gaps, they don't know that we put our snare there, so they get caught! And since they are not very smart, they pull until they can't pull no more. The end. Ptarmigan population control, and some fresh meat!" Atau's fingers walked through a snare, and it tightened around his wrist as he pulled away from it, eyes wide in a dramatic fashion. Piŋa laughed loudly at the performance, delight brightening his face.

The springtime memory of that day dissolved into the darkness of the eagles' hall. The smell of rotten bird brought him back to the present like a winter storm, overpowering the memory of the green willow buds. The echo of the laughter from that day stung the boy's eyes. *His* brothers. His smart, brave brothers. Killed by mythical beasts for some still mysterious and endless task. Piŋa frowned at the pile of ptarmigan feathers in front of him. Suddenly all he wanted was to be back there, following his brothers through the

willows. His chest ached with the need to have someone . . .
anyone . . . break through the deep snow for him to ease his
path forward.

*What if I am still too small, big brothers? What if it's too
deep for me to get through?*

11

HOLLOW

Two moons elapsed before the boy was deemed a passable maker of drums. Savik stopped meeting him in the mornings in the hall, leaving Piŋa on his own to practice all of the skills they taught him so far. The Eagle Mother would escort him in the mornings to his collection of drum-making supplies and then drift off again for her nap, waving her stick in the air in dismissal. She would come back in the evening to guide him back to his sleeping area. And so his days went.

This space of time between winter and spring was the most barren part of the year. The snow reluctantly gave way to reveal the pale, colorless ground beneath. What was once protected and insulated by deep layers of snow was scorched by the new sun, and even the hardiest of plants withered away to prepare for the growing season to come. This was the part of the year that food stores were likely to run out, even in prosperous times. And Piŋa was far from prosperous.

He carefully portioned out what food he had left. He slow-boiled what bones he could find in a shallow stone bowl over the seal-oil lamp he had in his room, trying his best to remove as many nutrients and as much residual fat as he could from the marrow and knuckles. He took care to check on his shrinking store of dried herbs and roots often, airing out any of the pieces that looked like they might become too damp and develop mold. But he hadn't been told what the next step was going to be, or even *when* it was going to be, and this uncertainty eroded his determination.

Eagle Mother ignored all of his polite questions. Eventually he took to asking her point-blank if he was done with his task and could go home. At first, she would answer him with brief words, saying that he needed to have patience, but after about a week of this routine, she just refused to answer him at all. Instead, she stabbed him with her stick until he quieted.

Days melted into one another. The feeling that he needed to be *doing something* grew and grew until he could almost physically feel it simmering and building. He found himself jumping from one emotion to another—frustration, sadness, anger, and exhaustion. Not knowing when this was going to end made him feel like he should be doing more. And slowly, that feeling spilled over and left him like an empty cup, and still he got no relief.

The hollowness in his chest grew and grew, fed by his loneliness, and soon it became a dark cavern that swallowed his days. All the songs he composed were songs of home. Sad and forlorn songs filled the eagles' hall with the helplessness of the boy's predicament. He could see the Eagle Mother and her brood watching him as he became more and more sullen, as he began sleeping in later and later into the day. He noticed his body became physically thinner and hunched over, but he couldn't really muster the energy to care about that very much. He could hear the eagles whisper about him from the darkness; they whispered to each other their guesses of what human ailment this could be, but after a while Piŋa figured that they left him to either recover on his own or die of whatever malady he might have. But even the whispering stopped after a while.

Savik assigned Isiġnaq to fly out and find plants for the boy, since he had exhausted the area around their home and it was bare from the change in seasons. Piŋa did his best to show her what to look for, but she was less than happy about it, so she went searching infrequently and avoided him whenever she could.

Now that the eagles left him mostly alone, he became even more desolate. At least before, his interactions with them gave him something to focus his energy on. Without them, Piŋa was like a fireweed seed tossed into the air, untethered and falling, not knowing where he was going to land.

12

LEMMING

There are many aspects of a sod building that contribute to its character: which direction the doorway faces, the size and placement of the window if there is one, how many rooms are built around the central space, the carvings on the arches or ivory carvings of protective animals buried into the sod itself. But one aspect is present in every single sod house in the Arctic: the lemmings.

The tiny, mouselike creatures are found in every sod house. They are the lowest on the food chain. Millions, billions of them feed the foxes, birds, wolves, and anything else with beak or bite. Sod houses provide protection against predators that are afraid of humans. And sod houses are always warm and cozy, with plenty of opportunities for lemmings to dig their burrows of tunnels and nests.

So when Piŋa first saw the lemming in the great hall, he didn't pay it much attention. He had had another tedious day of nothing except music practice while the eagles avoided him. The days cut at him like obsidian against grass with their slow emptiness.

The lemming sat just out of the boy's reach, watching Piŋa in his misery. Little dark eyes glittered in the half-light from the oil lamp. When the boy finally took notice and lifted his head to look at the little beast, anger burned across his face. His sadness was not a spectacle to be watched, especially by such a lowly creature. The boy wiped his tears and turned to look at the lemming directly, growling a bit under his breath, expecting the lemming to run when it realized it had been spotted.

But the lemming didn't run. It held its ground, small body trembling, as though it was fighting the instinct to flee. *Odd.* The boy stared directly into those tiny, dark eyes. The lemming was normal-looking for the most part. Its body was almost comically round, with tiny little brown limbs and a short tail, the usual dark stripe down its back,

and small ears almost invisible against its dense fur. But this one had a patch of pure white fur on its chest that glowed a little in the lamplight. Piŋa could see it clearly as the lemming sat on its hind legs.

The lemming squeaked at the boy. Not in fear or surprise. It was more of a question. Or at least what the boy thought a question would sound like if it was squeaked. The lemming turned its head a bit so that its other eye could get a better look.

Piŋa reached over, picked up one of his fur socks, and threw it as hard as he could at the lemming. His aim was true, and he hit the spot dead on where the lemming stood. Only, the lemming had guessed his move and jumped to the side. It still didn't run. Instead, the tiny beast took a few steps forward and sniffed the air, short whiskers waving at the boy as it leaned closer, as if perplexed by this boy and his particular scent, if lemmings could be perplexed. *Could lemmings be perplexed?*

"Get out of here," the boy said. He leaned forward and waved his hands in front of him.

The lemming snorted a tiny puff of air and turned its body. Making sure Piŋa was watching, the lemming closed its eyes and cocked its head. It was dismissive and oddly insulting. The boy was left staring at the slowly receding rear end of the lemming as it made its way down the hall.

Soon the lemming started showing up at Piŋa's workspace in the morning, sitting just at the edge of the lamplight. The boy could tell it was the same lemming by the white patch of fur on its chest. It would move around the room in stealthy silence from hiding place to hiding place, finding safe spots to observe the boy. At first the boy took some pleasure in chucking whatever item was close at hand at the lemming, and even got close to hitting it directly a few times. But eventually, curiosity won Piŋa over as the days went on and it continued to return. It was very unusual behavior for a lemming, who were normally shy and simple creatures.

One day the boy saved some food from his midmorning meal, a hand's length of masu, a sweet root that Isiġnaq had found for him during one of her flights somewhere off the mountain. He tossed it in the direction of the hiding lemming. The masu landed a short distance away from its twitching whiskers. The lemming slowly made its way to the offering, tiny furry nose sniffing the air as its dark eyes squinted at the boy. When it reached the root, it cautiously nibbled a piece off and ran back to the safety of the shadows, a brown blur streaking to the wall. A few minutes later the lemming came back, and this time it grabbed ahold of the entire root and awkwardly dragged it back to its hiding space, its tiny legs scrambling and flopping as it tried to move the giant root.

A small smile pulled at the corners of the boy's mouth. From that point on, the lemming followed Piŋa as soon as he was awake, always sticking to the shadows but hopeful for scraps. The boy tried his best to save food for the lemming, but what he received was scarce as it was, and the area around the hall was still bare from his own gathering. He decided to try to work toward getting more food for the lemming. After all, he was a good provider.

One evening, as Isiġnaq set down a wooden bowl of masu for his evening meal, the boy spoke to her quickly. "I know it's springtime, almost summer solstice probably. My mother digs for these roots, and I know they are the first plant to show up. I know plants. That is, I know what plants to pick. If you would let me pick plants for myself, if I can go outside the walls for a little, I can help out. I know you don't really like plants to eat. I can help."

The words came out of his mouth in a fumbling, awkward rush. Isiġnaq looked surprised at the request. The boy hadn't spoken to any of them for a while now. The eagle woman stared at him, eyes scanning him from head to toe, taking stock of his weak posture and pale skin. Her golden eyes narrowed a bit as her mouth wrinkled in thought. With two quick and wide steps, she was suddenly standing uncomfortably close to the boy. He could smell the wind on her clothes.

"Fine. There is a valley nearby, an hour away by foot. You can pick your plants once a week. I hate picking plants. I hate the dirt in my nails. I will watch you. And kill you if you try to escape, ai?" The boy nodded his head vigorously, keeping his gaze lowered, trying to look as harmless as possible. He wasn't sure about Isiġnaq's temperament, as she chose mostly to avoid him completely, and she'd never shown him any type of warmth. If she said she would kill him, then he believed her.

The first time he hiked to the valley, it took him almost two hours to reach it. Isiġnaq walked ahead of him, her long strides going up the rocky mountain soil in a fast pace. When she realized that he couldn't keep up, she slowed down, watching Piŋa carefully to make sure she wasn't pushing him beyond what his body could take. Being cooped up in the eagles' lair all winter with unpredictable food supplies had made him weak and out of shape. Now he was slow and needed to take frequent breaks. The trail was barely a trail at all, mostly a haphazard overgrown collection of old sheep footpaths that he had to navigate carefully. Eventually he found himself at the valley. It was shaped like a ladle, high in the mountains, fed by a slowly melting glacier at the handle end. This early in the season, there wasn't very much green in the valley, though the bare ground was peppered with the fuzzy, woolly baby itqiḷiaġruk plants and early buds of the masu that hinted at where to dig their roots.

He stood at the edge of the valley for a few moments, inhaling deeply, filling his lungs with air untainted by the smell of rotten bird. Muscles that were tense for months relaxed in the early spring sun, and he found himself enjoying the feeling of this new freedom he had.

13

STRANGERS

One early morning, Piŋa was awakened and told that he was to begin the third part of his training. It had been a few weeks since they had started letting him hike to the valley. Spring was in full swing, and with it came temperamental weather. Thick, heavy fog had prevented him from visiting the valley for a week, and he could feel the anxiety building up inside him again.

He got up quickly and grabbed his drum. The eagle family was waiting in their usual spot in the center of the great hall. But the boy noticed many shadowy figures sitting behind the family. As he got closer, he could tell there were men and women, from young adult age to a little younger than his parents, about ten of them altogether. They all wore parkas of different furs. Most wore nothing but wolf skins, while a few others wore only the smaller and darker wolverine skins. He could hear them murmuring as he entered the space.

Swallowing hard, the boy sat down quietly in front of the eagle family and kept his eyes low to the ground. Eagle Mother's voice rang out in the hall, startling him. She sounded stronger, though he could not say why.

"We will teach you how to uamit today. We have invited others to drum and sing so that we could be free to assist you, boy. Respect them, but do not speak to them. They are not here to socialize." She turned and gestured to Savik and Nautchiaq.

Savik stood up and removed his parka, revealing a broad and slightly shimmering chest. Nautchiaq also stood up and removed her parka; heavy beads of amber, jade, and ivory hung low on her neck. Her hair had been braided into short loops, and more beads hung at the ends of the braids. On her hands she wore long, pointed mittens with tufts of soft white rabbit fur at the very tips. Savik had put on gloves sporting dangles on their backs made from pieces of ivory, bone, and wood that clinked when he moved. The two stood in front of the group, a couple of arms' lengths between them. Savik flexed his hands and spread his feet wider than his shoulders. Nautchiaq bowed her head demurely, feet close together and knees slightly bent, arms held out loosely to her sides.

The people behind them started drumming and singing, quietly at first. Most just hummed along to the faint drumbeats, and some of the drum strikes were out of beat as everyone worked to find the same rhythm. The sound grew louder and louder as they aligned with one another, filling all the empty space. Each round of drumbeats grew upon the last round, till the complicated layers urged their own blood to mimic the fast pace. The air crackled with suspense.

Nautchiaq's arms rose, and she held them up as if she were a great eagle in flight, her movements graceful and soft. Her knees bent in time with the drum, as though the drumbeats became a draft that she balanced on.

Savik spread his legs wider, his right foot keeping time with the beat. He lifted his arms and pointed his fists upward, head cocked and bobbing with confidence. He kept his head high, and the boy could see pure joy transforming the man's face, so unlike his normal scowl. As the words, drums, and movements came together, the boy felt a powerful sound vibrating the bones in his body.

I saw and circled him

Nautchiaq with wings spread glided around Savik.

Aa ya yai ai yaa
He was proud and smart

Savik looked down, then up, with a fist, shaking his hands, rattling the beads on his gloves.

Aa ya yai ai yaa
I asked him to leave with me

Nautchiaq gracefully beckoned with a pointed hand, tufts of white fur floating in the air.

Aa ya yai ai yaa
He would not leave

Savik shook his head and turned his body away.

His parents would mourn

Savik hid his face in the crook of his elbow.

Aa ya yai ai yaa
Eagle takes the man and they fight!

Nautchiaq grabbed Savik's elbow and circled him. Savik screamed in defiance.

He is brave!
But the eagle is strong!

They continued to struggle against each other, pulling one way, then the other. Their motions were tense and precise, faces beaded with sweat and taut with concentration. The sharp sound of Nautchiaq's beads combined with the dangles on Savik's gloves added to the frantic nature of the story, emphasizing each and every movement.

Aa ya yai ai ya ya ya
The man is defeated, but the eagle cries!

Nautchiaq cried out loud like an eagle, releasing Savik, who fell to his knees, head tilted up. Savik shook his gloves at his side, the rattling noise an eerie hiss that faded along with the song.

Aa ya yai ai yaa

Aa ya yai ai yaa

When the song was over, the boy stared at them, eyes wide as he tried to wrap his mind around the story that he had just experienced. A few people cleared their throats or rubbed oil into their drums in the silence. Savik and Nautchiaq made their way back to their mother's side and sat down.

They had shown him what had happened between Maliġu and Savik. Piŋa knew he was being shown Maliġu's death. He knew from what Savik told him that Atau fought immediately, and his second brother had refused to go with him. Maliġu had known that it was foolhardy to go up against Savik in his eagle form, but he had, nevertheless, chosen that ending. Savik had perfectly mimicked Maliġu's wide stance and strong, deliberate movements that Piŋa remembered so well. There were no tears of mourning, there was no tightness in his throat. Instead, the boy raised his head and looked Savik straight in the eyes. It was a sign of disrespect, he knew. But Savik returned his gaze for a moment before returning his attention to his mother.

The boy wondered why they had shown him this. The dance felt like a threat, or maybe like a reminder, to not refuse them, that they would let nothing stand between them and their goal. Maybe they thought they were giving him a gift, showing his brother's bravery. Maybe they were mocking him and his brothers. Whatever their goal, it made a shiver of cold walk down his spine, and he promised himself then and there not to forget what they were and where he was at.

The Eagle Mother tapped her stick on the hard-packed ground in front of her, the sound bringing him back to the present.

"Dancing brings a story to life, boy," the old woman said. "It brings songs to life." *Her voice is stronger,* thought the boy. "You will learn all that we know about dancing."

Later that night, when he was alone and the sounds of people moving in the dark hall stilled, Piŋa pulled himself out from his sleeping mat and sat on top of it. Sleep would not come tonight. He could still hear the song about Malġu's last moments in his head, and each drumbeat drove sleep further and further away. He dug into his food stash and pulled out the driest of the sweet roots he could find and rolled it around his mouth. The sharp edges of the root bit into his tongue and cheeks. He was hoping the small amount of pain would distract him from his thoughts of his brother as it softened enough to eat. But even then, he could still hear Savik's foot, pounding in time with the drum.

A sleepy-sounding squeak brought him back to the present. Lemming stood in the corner, whiskers twitching as it sniffed the air. Piŋa smiled and reached into his food stash again and brought out another piece of root, this one fat and not even a little bit shriveled. He tossed it at the lemming, who came closer and began nibbling on the food, tiny bright eyes watching the boy carefully.

"Do you want to hear what Malġu was really like, little lemming?" he said as he leaned closer, pitching his voice so he wouldn't wake anyone up. He started with his mother's stories first, how Malġu could carry a caribou for miles without tiring. The sound of his memories drowned out the echo of the drumbeats.

The next morning, the group of strangers were already in the great hall ahead of him, rubbing oil into the stretched skin of their drums, striking them to test the tone. The air smelled of fresh seal blubber and melting frost. As Piŋa sat down, he took some time to study them closer in the lamplight. He could tell from their faces and the angry tone of their conversations that floated across to him that they weren't very happy to be there. Every once in a while, they would shoot him or the eagles angry looks that he pretended he didn't see. Why were they so angry? And what did that anger mean for him?

The morning started out rough. He was instructed to strip down to just his short caribou leggings and stand in front of the drummers, in between Savik and Nautchiaq. The cool early summer air drifted through the open windows and made him shiver. His pale skin and slight body stood in contrast to the heavily muscled Savik, and some of the drummers chuckled quietly as they exchanged glances and gestured at him. He crossed his arms in front of himself and turned toward Savik, suddenly embarrassed. He felt exposed and unbalanced, which he knew everyone could readily see.

"The children's dance." Savik gestured at the drummers and singers, requesting the song, which made them chuckle again. The boy blushed as all eyes turned to them. "Watch me and Nautchiaq to see the differences and similarities in how men and women dance. This first dance is easy. We will do it over and over till you get it."

The song was simple, with no changes in beat, no pauses, and it didn't even have words, just a repetitive sound phrase sung over and over. The boy watched the first two short rounds of the dance carefully and then tried his best to mimic Savik. His couldn't get his movements in time with the beat no matter what he did, and his arms struck out at odd angles and flailed around like fish tossed onto dry land. His feet stuttered trying to mimic Savik's smooth, effortless foot stomps.

Savik grabbed the boy's arms and lifted them higher.

"Focus on the arms first. Learn the beginning movements first, then add some more, and so on. Don't try to do it all at first. Kiita. Let's go."

He tried his best. But his coordination was poor, and since Piŋa couldn't see what his own movements looked like, Savik had to move his arms about like a puppet, which only added to the humiliation.

When Savik ended their lesson, Piŋa was escorted back to his corner, where he slumped down onto his sleeping fur. His arms were heavy and throbbed in pain. Muscles he didn't even know he had ached and made him wince with every movement. He dug himself deeper into his sleeping furs, barely touching the food the sisters brought him. What little sleep he got that night was troubled, and he dreamed of wolves chasing him through deep snow that clung at his arms and legs, dragging him down.

Ten days later, during one of the many breaks the boy needed, Piŋa sat off to the side with his back to the drummers, rubbing a cramping calf. He no longer shook with fatigue from dancing, and he found if he worked the knots out of his muscles early on, he could avoid most of the soreness the next day. Savik had gone to get water.

"Maybe the eagles should have picked a more fit *pup* to do all this, ah? It must be hard because you're so . . . tiny."

Piŋa spun around quickly, startled by the unfamiliar voice. The man in the black wolf skins was crouched near him, eyes boring into his own, mouth in an exaggerated pucker as he looked the boy up and down. The muscles in the boy's jaw tightened at the double insult. The man flashed his unnaturally white teeth in an unfriendly grin. The man moved in closer, uncomfortably close, so close that Piŋa noticed his teeth were slightly pointed. Piŋa tried to lean away a little, and when he did, the man's smile grew.

The man slammed his hand down on the ground, the sound making the boy flinch. Piŋa glanced around the room and realized that there were no eagles within immediate earshot. Several of the other drummers openly watched with interest, but none of them intervened.

The boy gestured at his calf, and strained to say politely, "Muscles can grow and, very painfully, become fit. But yeah, I am small." Piŋa raised his eyebrows in agreement and plastered a smile on his face, hoping it looked natural. Hoping his face didn't betray his sudden nervousness.

The grin left the man's face. Piŋa could smell the musky scent of his wolf-skin parka. This close, he could see that the man was underweight, his cheeks were hollow, and his hands clasped in front of him were thin and wiry. The gauntness of his body added to the man's unfriendly presence. His lip curled a little as he spoke.

"The eagles think you are so special. I don't think you are that special," he hissed, sending tiny flecks of spittle in Piŋa's direction. The boy kept his eyes averted from the man's face, hoping it would help him seem less confrontational. He raised his eyebrows in a silent acknowledgment while he frantically tried to figure out what to do. His heart pounded in his chest.

Why is this man so angry?

Even underweight, Piŋa knew this man could hurt him if he wanted to. What would happen if he did get hurt? What would happen if he fought back?

"I don't think I am that special, either," the boy admitted while nodding, hoping a little humility would defuse the situation. The man leaned away from him, eyes narrowed. Then he stood up quickly, walking away from Piŋa and sitting down with the rest of the group seconds before Savik emerged from the front of the house. The boy sighed heavily in relief upon seeing Savik, who frowned in his direction, sensing the tension.

Unbelievable! Piŋa thought. *I am* relieved *to see the eagle?*

He felt nauseous from the encounter. He could still feel eyes on his back. What did they think about him? Were they all angry? He had never had to imagine what a stranger would be thinking. He had never treated anyone like that man had treated him and could not imagine what would make him so bitter.

He could not read minds, and so it seemed like the anger would always be a consequence of meeting new people. A memory drove itself to the surface of his mind.

14

PATHS

When he was around ten years old, while walking to their wintering grounds, Piŋa and his family crested a hill and were startled to find another family on the other side of it, huddled around a small fire shielded from the wind. They all froze midstride. They were close enough that he could see the surprised looks on the faces of the strangers, how the whites around their eyes glowed against dark skin. There were two men, two women, and a group of children of differing ages. The boy stood in place, surprised by the fear that flooded his body. He had never been this close to other people before.

Two of the kids were about his age, a boy and girl who

he only got a quick glimpse before one of the women pulled them behind the men. The strange men immediately stood and reached for their weapons, drawing deadly obsidian tips pointed at his family. His father and brothers stepped in front of him and his mother, and they also drew their weapons. The air was as taut as a bowstring. He could feel the tension on his skin.

One of the strange men stepped forward slowly and waved the short spear he was carrying in front of him. "We are too poor for you to rob, we will move on," he said in a gruff voice, shouting across the space between them. His speech was oddly accented. "Surely such rich people as yourself have no need for what we have."

Rich? At his words, the boy looked at the strangers more closely and saw that yes, their clothes were of lesser quality than his family's, though they were well made and patched expertly. He also noted that none of them had the decorative trim that his mother loved making for his family.

"We are only passing through and saw some good hunting. We are low on food."

His father used the tip of his seal spear to gesture to his right, away from the strange family. "Yes, we will part, then." Mother grabbed Piŋa's upper arm tightly and led him away.

His brothers followed close, glancing behind them often, gripping their spears with white knuckles. Father followed last, his face alert, only relaxing once they were out of the immediate area and he could see they were not followed. Father stopped Malġu and directed him to hide himself along their trail, to make sure the strangers left. Atau jogged ahead of them to make sure they did not get surprised by anyone else.

Piŋa couldn't understand why his family was so fearful. The strangers looked rough, worn, and a little hungry, but why did Father believe they were dangerous? It was obvious Piŋa's family was the stronger group.

Later that evening, as they gathered around the fire, Piŋa brought up the subject to his father and asked why they were so afraid of those people. Father sat in silence for a while, gathering his thoughts. Mother for once was quiet and also would not meet his eyes.

"People are different, iġñiin. They are raised different; they experience different things, have different luck. We know ourselves, but we can never know strangers that well. We don't know what kind of people they are. We don't know at what point they will not be friends and what would make them turn on us. It is best to avoid the vulnerability in the long run."

The boy sat in silence. That night he lay for a long time in his bed, staring at the flickering wick of the single large seal-oil lamp, thoughts tangled like his mother's hair when she woke up. His family slept around him in a protective circle. They had made it back to the sod house on their wintering grounds without incident. Everyone had fallen asleep quickly, exhausted from the tension from seeing the strange family. Everyone but Piŋa.

Quietly he stood up, making sure to cause as little sound as possible as he ducked through the tunnel entrance into the cool weather of late summer. He moved as quickly as he could down the farthest siġḷuaq ladder, emerging with a skin pouch full of dried seal meat preserved in seal oil. The sides of the pouch were slick with melting frost. He struggled to keep a good grip, so at first he didn't see the fur-clad feet at the top of the ladder. When he stood up, he was confronted by his oldest brother. Atau looked annoyed, hair lopsided in an untidy mess, sleep still at the corners of his eyes.

"Father woke me up and told me to go and fetch you. Thought you would be doing something unwise." He raised his eyebrows and nodded at the pouch that the boy was still trying to hold. "Are you doing something like that, little brother? Or are you getting a huge meal ready for all of us to eat in the middle of the night? If you grab a small bag of greens from near the ladder, it will be a good meal, or else it will be too rich." The boy's face reddened, and he pulled his arms tighter around the pouch. He didn't answer.

His brother sighed and rubbed his face with his large-knuckled hands, then sat down cross-legged on a patch of tundra a little higher than the rest of the ground. He waved a hand at the boy and gestured for him to sit.

"Piŋa, sit down. There is another reason Father sent me. I once tried doing what you are doing now, when I was about the same age, maybe a little older. Except I got a lot farther than you did. Father didn't catch me till I got to them—to another band of strangers we had spotted from a distance. I could tell they were hungry, too. It was an older couple with many children. I thought that if we could help them, I would have someone to play with besides my quiet, slow brother, Malġu." He smiled and waited as the boy placed the pouch down and settled himself on the ground.

"I actually talked to them a little, too, before Father got there. I guess he wanted me to tell you what happened." Piŋa's ears perked up, surprised to hear a story he had never heard before. His brother reached over and plucked a few tundra-grass stalks expertly from a nearby tussock so that the tender pink base of the plants was intact. He chewed on them slowly, letting the tart flavor of the plant fill his mouth.

"Yeah, I made it to those people. I thought maybe they would be wary of me at first, but then they would be happy I brought them food, you know? Then we could be friends. But that is not what happened, little baby brother. No. They wanted to know why I had brought them food. I told them because they looked hungry. They asked me what I wanted in return, and said that they had nothing to offer since they were so poor. I said I wanted nothing in return, except maybe some stories or just friendship. But this only made them angry; they thought I was hiding something. Maybe my father and brother were waiting to ambush them once I gained their trust, they said. The more I tried to reassure them, the more they thought I was lying. I don't know why. Maybe I talked too much, maybe not enough. Maybe I said the wrong things. I was young and foolish." He smiled at Piŋa and handed him some tundra-grass stalks to chew on. Atau stared off in the direction of the sun slowly trying to rise. The sky was turning a deep purple, and the stars began disappearing one by one. The boy chewed his grass stalk, waiting for his brother to start talking again.

"Anyway, luckily Father came and got me before it got ugly. And Father never really brought it up, but of course I never tried to talk to strangers again." He snorted, gesturing at the pouch the boy had brought up from the siġluaq. Piŋa pulled the chewed-up stalk of grass from his mouth and wrapped it around his fingers as he thought about what his brother had just told him. Soon the stalk was nothing but kinks and bends and torn threads, as he worked through his thoughts that were also a mess of kinks and bends.

Atau stared at his youngest brother in the brightening light of day, his face serious. "But if you want to go and see those people, baby brother, I will come with you. I would have your back."

The boy glanced back at his family's sod house. Soon his parents and Malġu would be getting up to start the day. He briefly scrunched his nose. "No. Not today, anyway." Atau raised his brows and stood up to dust off the tundra leaves clinging to his pants.

As Piŋa entered the sod house, he thought of the strangers and the way they waved their spears. Would there be a day, though?

15

CONNECTIONS

Piŋa danced every day. His body grew limber, and his muscles became strong again over the next two moons. He learned how to avoid the young man with angry eyes and made sure an eagle was nearby at all times, in case the man decided to attack. Soon the mountaintop was carpeted by early summertime plants, the tiny, fuzzy itqiḷiaġruk flowers bloomed their sweet-smelling pink flowers, and the low-growing willows were covered in their equally fuzzy blooms. They seemed to be fighting for the attention of the slow-flying bumblebees that had finally emerged. Piŋa worked hard to gather as much of the new growth as possible, preserving the green willow leaves and the itqiḷiaġruk and masu roots in seal fat brought to him by the eagles.

The air was warm and thick with mosquitoes and biting flies, though he noticed they were less bothersome this high up in the mountains. He was instructed to create his own dances to prove his mastery. He worked through some songs that he had created earlier and molded dance movements to them. He took inspiration from his family. One was a walrus hunting song based on his father's stories. Another was about his brother Malġu carrying a whole caribou home across his shoulders for two miles. And a couple were about his two brothers teaching him how to trap ptarmigan in the spring.

When he demonstrated all of the dances and songs to a stone-faced Savik, the eagle man gestured at the drummers. Most of them were unimpressed and barely paying attention. Some quietly chatted with one another, waiting for a signal to start drumming again.

"A big part of dancing is being able to teach the dance. You need to see the song from both ends, creator and learner." Savik's voice then got louder as he turned and addressed the drummers. "Who among you would want to learn this boy's song?" All of their eyes turned toward Piŋa, and the quiet conversations stopped immediately. None of the drummers moved or made a sound. Savik's brow furrowed as the silence stretched on. The boy's heart was pounding as the familiar feeling of vulnerability swept over him. "Two volunteers, a man and a woman, are needed to help this boy learn to teach. Ai?"

The drummers looked at one another. An older woman stood up from the back of the group. She was about his mother's age, though smaller. She moved quietly toward the front of the group. Her face was sharp-featured and stern, and a thin, pale scar stretched across her chin in a curving arc. She reached an arm above and behind her in a practiced move and removed her parka, revealing a sleeveless shirt made of sun-bleached leather.

Another figure stood up, and the boy's heart sank when he saw it was the angry young man. As he removed his parka, the boy could see in the dim light that the man's dark skin was peppered with small scars. It looked like a hundred tiny wounds, deep enough to make a scar but not enough to be life-threatening. The boy stared at them for a moment, wondering what could cause such cuts. The man chuckled and slapped his chest, a wide grin on his face. "Not a little boy's skin, ami."

The boy looked at Savik, hoping that he would see the tension. Hoping he would see it and pick another person.

Savik frowned at both of them for a moment, grunted, and nodded at the boy to begin.

Piŋa realized then that he was meant to be challenged. That this angry man was to be part of his lessons.

Savik stepped back and found a caribou skin on the floor to sit on and watch. The hall was silent as all eyes looked to them. The boy swallowed the dryness in his throat.

"What should I call you? Your names?" Piŋa asked them.

"You can call me Pula. They say my scar looks like the sun during an eclipse." The woman's voice was just as small and quiet as she was, and he had to strain to hear what she said.

"You can call me . . . Alik," the man said, gesturing at the many small scars on the skin of his chest and back. He chuckled a little as the boy found himself looking at them again. "Get it? Little tears all over. Holes all over." His smile held no humor in it. The boy frowned at the angry man. How was he supposed to work with a man who hated him? What was his problem? *Why not just ask?*

"Why are you so angry at me, Alik? Why work with me if you don't like me?"

The man's lip curled, but instead of answering, he looked at Savik, who crossed his arms, offering no support for either one of them. Alik looked back at the boy, pushing his shoulders up as he balled his fists. He stepped forward, making the boy lean away. "I don't like how you smell, boy."

The boy looked away quickly and bent to pick up his drum, trying to hide his nervousness. *Well, that didn't solve anything.*

He paused for a moment, glancing at Savik and then back at Alik and Pula, wondering what exactly was going through their minds.

Right then he decided to do a different song and dance. He had planned to teach them a dance he had made about hunting walrus, which he was particularly fond of because of its complexity, and he wanted to impress everyone. But he changed his mind as he felt the open hostility radiate from Alik and the indifference from Pula. He needed something simpler. He adjusted the weight of the drum in his hands as his palms started to sweat. Mentally he went through the list of dances and songs he had created, searching for one that would fit this moment. His hands grazed the drum. The rough sinew binding scratched at the skin between his thumb and pointer finger. Even with all the practice he got making sinew here in the eagles' nest, he still didn't have enough patience to make it as smooth and strong as his mother could make it. His mother's face popped into his mind; her gentle, patient smile warmed his heart, dispelling some of the nervousness. He missed the sound of her voice. Her nonstop talking. At least he never wondered what she was thinking.

Feeling inspired by the memory, he picked his song and started to talk.

"My first memory in my life is of my mother. When I was really young, she would pack me on her back and then set me on the ground to watch her pick plants that were in season. She would talk nonstop about it: their names as they changed, what to do with the plants, and things like that. My earliest childhood memory was her voice and those plants. I could not understand what she was saying—you know, the actual words—but the rhythm of her voice while picking really stuck with me." The boy paused and looked at their faces. Pula had a small smile on her face, and Alik looked at least a little less hostile. Perhaps they were thinking of their own mothers. "I hope you will let me teach you?"

He looked again at Pula and Alik. Both raised their eyebrows to signal yes. Pula smiled even brighter, and said, "My mother liked to eat sweet roots sometimes. She was really good at finding them in the early spring."

Alik sighed and looked away from the boy. "Doesn't everyone's mother do that, though?" He grunted at Piŋa, but the boy noticed a gentler tone. It was a start.

Piŋa thought his mother would be proud of him for talking.

The boy sang the song a few times with the drummers, until they could repeat it easily. Then he turned his attention to Alik and Pula. He demonstrated each section of the dance with exaggerated movements, repeating them over and over. The dance was simple, with movements of walking while searching the ground, plucking plants and storing them, gentle arcs that represented the turning of the seasons, and finally eating the plants. It turned out that Pula and Alik were quick learners. They even suggested a few changes to the performance that the boy welcomed. When they were done, Savik seemed satisfied. They concluded their session, and everyone split up to find a meal.

"Tell me, what did you learn today, boy?" Savik asked. It was unusual for the man to ask the boy to reflect on his day, so Piŋa thought he must be looking for something specific. The boy paused while putting away his drums and sat thinking. He knew Savik wasn't asking about teaching the dance; he was asking about how Piŋa had interacted with two strangers.

He scratched his forehead as the sweat from dancing dried into a layer that tightened his skin. He made a mental note to find some moss so that he could bathe.

"I learned not to lead with demands. I learned to lead with connections. And next time I will remember that not everyone will like me, but not everyone has to like me to fulfill a goal."

"Smart boy." Savik grunted and slapped Piŋa on the back as he rose and went to do whatever the eagle did at night.

16

LESSONS

Piŋa sat with the Eagle Mother, tending to the skin on a small drum, gently rubbing the surface with a small amount of seal oil.

"You ever wonder where the north wind comes from?" he asked. "Why it's so cold? I have always wondered why it's so different from the other winds." He paused for a response, then sighed when she continued to completely ignore him.

The drummers, along with Pula and Alik, had long since left to go back to wherever they had come from. Summer began to fade, and hints of fall dulled the vibrant color of all of the green plants. The orange aqpik berries carpeted the boggy nooks of the mountains and would be ripe soon.

The caribou meat the eagles brought him was thick again with fat. It had been almost a year since arriving here at the mountaintop. Even then, time seemed to go a little slower here in the eagles' home, like walking through water, the seasons stretching forever. Piŋa and the Eagle Mother were alone this morning, and she had been ignoring him and his feeble attempts at conversation. He was uncomfortable, as usual, with the eagles' habit of sitting unmoving in complete silence. Was it a type of meditation, maybe? Perhaps they were waiting for some signal he could not sense. Maybe they could hear something he could not. Her clothing rustled as she moved.

"A few short lessons, boy, and then you can go home."

The boy turned from the drum he had in his hands and met the eyes of the Eagle Mother. He thought for sure he had misheard her. Could his time with the eagles finally be ending soon? He looked down at his slick, calloused hands and was silent for a moment, letting the statement sink into his mind as the oil soaked into his skin. The smallest trickle of hope bloomed in his chest, like a wick being lit on his mother's seal-oil lamp, hesitant and warm.

"Springtime." He bargained. "I can learn it all by the time spring starts warming the mountains in eight moons."

She smiled, and this time the boy was able to see her smile more clearly. *Are there fewer wrinkles than before? How strange*, he thought.

"It will hopefully be quicker than that. Come outside, boy, and we will begin." The Eagle Mother slowly stood up from her pile of furs. They walked toward the entrance.

The boy hesitated at the door. He had continued to go out to the hidden valley with Isiġnaq watching from the skies, but it felt different somehow with the Eagle Mother. He took a deep breath and cautiously followed Eagle Mother.

The day was bright and warm. The constant wind carried the scent of summer in quick retreat on its back. He could see a couple of eagles in human form outside their sod houses, tending to skins and meat hanging on drying racks, taking advantage of the breeze. The boy followed the Eagle Mother as she strode along the outside of the great hall, dragging the tip of her stick across the tightly packed sod. The sod was old. He could tell by how the grass had grown thick, weaving an airtight seal. Small white flowers emerged from its bulk; they filled the air with the smell of sugary sap that tickled his nose.

When Piŋa and Eagle Mother reached the back of

the hall, they came upon Savik, who was crouched down, arranging some strange objects on the ground. As they got closer, Eagle Mother stopped and gestured for the boy to sit opposite Savik. He did so with haste, knowing better than to test their patience today. He didn't want to make them angry and have them storm off, in the usual eagle fashion. No, no games today, not when he held the hope of going home soon.

Savik offered a thin smile at Piŋa's obvious enthusiasm, eyebrows raised. "I thought a little air would do you good, boy," he said. He waved at the ground in front of him. "Examine these things."

Cautiously, the boy leaned over and peered at the ground. In the center was a small mound that was cut in half so that he could see that it was hollow and held up by pale curved sticks that resembled rib bones. On top of the bones were arranged tiny slabs of what looked like . . . sod. The boy gasped. "It's a tiny sod house!" he said.

Savik nodded at the miniature building. "It is called a qalgi, boy. It is a place to sing and dance . . . and feast. You will learn how to build this sod house large enough for a hundred people to fit inside." The boy's eyes widened. He had helped his father and mother rebuild a part of their sod

house before, mostly just doing the heavy work of hauling wood and slabs of sod, but he knew nothing about building a structure the size of the eagles' great hall.

The boy looked at the tiny model in front of him and wiped at the moisture that beaded on the bridge of his nose, grasping the enormity of the task before him. How long would it take for him to learn such a thing? There was no way he could build it before freeze-up. And what if he failed? He wasn't a great builder. Not like his brothers before him. Not like his parents. His mind had just never worked that way, couldn't picture things in his head before he built them. Not complex things, anyway. He thought with horror, *What if it collapses?*

"Why would I need such a large building? Are we to live with your kind?"

Eagle Mother grunted and walked away, back toward the entrance of the hall. Well, it hadn't taken him long to annoy at least one eagle. Piŋa looked back at Savik, who dismissed his question with a wave of his hand. If only his self-doubt could be so easily dismissed.

The boy sat closer to the little model. Savik began pulling out more little pieces of bone and sod and wood from a pile behind him. He tossed them in front of the boy.

"First you will make a model yourself, to get a feel for the weight distribution and to build the image in your mind. Then we will build a hall with you in that little valley you like so much, the one Isiġnaq takes you to dig your plants. Not as large as our home, but something that will do for our purposes."

The afternoon went downhill from there. It didn't matter that Savik explained, many times, how the little building was to be constructed, the relationship between the angles and weight and lengths. It all sounded like gibberish to Piŋa. He could understand the words, but when Savik put them together, they suddenly became a puzzle he could not solve. When Savik started talking about the force, or something pushing down, and how it needed to be dispersed, he might as well have been chittering to the boy in his eagle form. The boy just sat there without responding, frustration making him silent.

Eventually Savik got annoyed, his face red and nostrils flaring as he started to yell, as if that would help the boy finally understand. And for the second time that day, an eagle stomped off in annoyance. Not the boy's best effort. Piŋa stayed in the clearing for a while longer, fiddling with the tools Savik had left behind and feeling like a fool. He couldn't understand it with a teacher, much less on his own. The first of his qalgi lessons ended shortly after that. The boy returned to his corner inside the hall earlier than usual, defeated. Isiġnaq brought him a roasted piece of caribou hindquarter for dinner. She looked just about as pleased as Savik had. He was certain she set down the wooden platter harder than she usually did. He imagined everyone had heard Savik and him yelling at each other all day.

Annoyed with himself and needing something to stop the feeling of helplessness sneaking into his mind, the boy dug around his shelves and pulled out a small leather pouch filled with ippiq leaves. They were tightly packed one on top of the other to prevent the air from making them spoil too fast. He didn't have seal oil to store them in and had run out of caribou fat, so he had to eat the thin, leathery leaves before they went bad. As he placed the leaves on his tongue, their tart taste made his mouth water immediately. Thinking of seal oil brought his father to mind. His father took care in how he harvested seals. He always offered the seal's spirit the gift of fresh water, and he made sure to cut the seal's body so that death did not taint the taste of the blubber and meat. Like everything his father did, he did it with deliberation and patience and knowledge. Piŋa wished he possessed even a small amount of his father's calm and forethought when it came to building.

A small piping squeak interrupted his thoughts. He searched for the sound and found the tiny lemming, white spot of fur glowing on its chest, standing on its back legs, whiskers sniffing at the air. The boy tossed a few of the leaves in its direction, eager for the company.

"Hello, lemming. Glad to see you." The lemming squeaked, the sound muffled as it chewed the ippiq into smaller pieces and stuffed its cheek pouches full. The boy smiled for a moment, and then his face darkened again. "Do you know how to build a great hall, little lemming? Can you teach me?" He asked this, not expecting an answer. All he heard in response was the sound of loud rodent chewing.

He turned to take his knife and cut off a piece of the caribou meat, then popped the chunk in his mouth. When he looked back, the lemming was gone.

17

LEMMING HALL

The next morning, Piŋa woke up long before the eagles. Anxiety had swirled around his mind all night, slow and murky, and it had refused to let him sleep very long. What sleep he got was plagued with dreams of running across the tundra, feet moving as fast as they could, but when he looked around, he realized that no matter how hard he ran, he was stuck in the same place. The feeling of helplessness followed him into the waking world. He sat and waited to be collected by the Eagle Mother, watching as the distant light from the sun streamed in through the opened skylights, turning from a cool blue to warm, dust-filled beams.

Today I am going to try. *If I can learn to dance and sing, then I can learn this.*

While he waited, he dug out some more ippiq greens from his pouch and layered them with slivers of dried fish from another pouch. The fatty fish melted in his mouth, combining pleasantly with the green, tart taste of the leaves. He washed everything down with gulps from his water pouch.

Piŋa looked around his corner and took in his small collection of drums. His eyes moved over to a rabbit-skin tunic and caribou-skin mittens hanging from the wall, and then to his worn-out sealskin boots and small pouches of dried plants and meat. He had made all of these things. If he could make it this far with so little, then surely he could learn how to build a qalgi.

A squeak came from the dark, and the boy smiled and turned toward the sound.

"Can't say no to a free meal?" he said as he tossed some leaves to the little lemming. The creature dashed from the shadows and collected the food, disappearing just as Eagle Mother showed up to escort him. They made their way back outside, where Savik was waiting, angry frown and all. Eagle Mother put her face close to Piŋa's, meeting him eye to eye as she searched his face for a few moments. The smell of dusty rot surrounded him. He prepared himself to keep a straight face so that she didn't see him react to her smell this close, but he was surprised that it no longer stung his nose. He must have gotten used to it. She made a low growling noise in her throat.

"Boy, you need to connect somehow to these lessons, to make the information fit into your head. Try harder. If you can't, we might have to move on and find someone more capable." And with that she turned abruptly and shuffled back to the entrance of her hall. Her last words echoed in his head. How could they not understand that he was trying? Piŋa sat across from Savik on the ground, watching him arrange curved pieces of wood into a low arch over a slight depression in the ground.

Savik spoke. "Again. Only about half of the qalgi is actually aboveground. Some of it is below. The part that is aboveground needs to be adjusted for size and width and height. The key to building any structure is the allocation of weight. Sod is heavy, and it becomes heavier with moisture and snow. The weight pushes down and out. That pressure has to be met with equal amounts of weight along the sides and walls, as well as an adequate arch of bone across the top."

Savik gestured to the arch he had made and the slabs of

sod on the sides. The boy looked at the model closely, noting as many of the details as he could, but he wasn't too sure what he was supposed to be looking at. It just looked like a pile of dirt held up by some spindly sticks and fake little whale bones. Savik then placed a large flat rock the length of his forearm on top of the small model structure and released it. The structure held, to Piŋa's amazement. Savik reached over after a few minutes, removed the rock, and dismantled the tiny structure. He smoothed the depression out so that the ground was flat. "Now rebuild that section you just saw, so that it can carry the weight of the rock."

Swallowing hard, the boy did as he was told. He made a shallow hole in the dirt and placed the sticks and bones as close to what he could remember as possible. When he was vaguely satisfied with what he had built, he looked at Savik, who gestured to the rock. The boy picked up the rock, which was heavier than he thought, and tried to place it as slowly as he could onto the structure he had built. The rock immediately crushed his efforts, not even offering any type of resistance.

"Your base was too narrow; your arch was too high. Try again." Savik grunted. Piŋa nodded. Swallowing his frustration, he propped up the pieces again. He spread the miniature bones farther apart than the first time by a couple of inches. This made the arch much lower. He picked up the rock as Savik watched, and placed it on the little building again. The tiny bones were instantly crushed, shooting out from beneath the rock. One landed near Savik.

"Too far apart that time. Try again," Savik said, tossing the piece back. Piŋa gathered all the pieces together and started over. This time he was sure that he got it right. He placed the rock on top and held his breath. Everything tilted to the side, immediately crushing his efforts.

"One side was higher than the other; the weight shifted to the lower side. Try again."

Piŋa turned to him, fists balled and shoulders hunched.

"I am doing exactly what you tell me to do. Why don't you just explain what I am supposed to be looking for, instead of ordering me about," the boy said through gritted teeth. "I don't know what you mean by 'distribution of weight' and 'height' or any of that stuff. I'm not good with that type of thing. Give me a target to hit with my bow and arrow and I can hit it. But this stuff makes no sense to me!"

Savik stood up, and the boy expected the usual yelling. Instead, the man spun around stiffly and walked off. The boy could hear him grumbling angrily as he walked away.

Piŋa slumped to the ground and rubbed his face with his hands, trying to figure out what to do next.

He had never thought of himself as someone capable of failure. He could run for long distances, walk even longer, and was better than his brothers and father at hitting a target with any type of weapon. His trapping skills were more than adequate, and he could create and care for tools, even in his sleep. He had met the challenges of learning how to craft beautiful drums, dance for hours, and compose complex songs quicker than he even thought possible. He had always excelled in all of the tasks he was given and all that was asked of him by his parents. Always.

Thinking of his parents brought back memories of them building the sod house they lived in. It was quite a few years ago, and he vaguely remembered the process. Even then he had not been excited about it all. He remembered hauling a ton of sod, walking the beaches looking for washed-up bones, and dragging back large driftwood logs with the dogs. He had not been involved much with the actual planning and building of the internal structure. He wondered if his parents understood that he didn't really have the knack for that type of work and just never pushed him. He wished he had paid more attention to what they were doing then.

He rubbed his eyes with the tips of his fingers, watching the inside of his eyelids sparkle with pinpoints of light. How was he to get through this?

A familiar small squeak got his attention, and he opened his eyes to see the lemming sitting in front of him. The tiny creature sniffed at the air and darted to the crushed model that the boy had made. The boy sighed and picked up a stick, digging its tip into the dirt in front of him.

"I don't have food, little friend. Maybe later."

The lemming squeaked again. Piŋa looked up and was surprised to see that behind the lemming a section of the ground was...moving. That was what it looked like at first. The brown mass of dirt drifted toward him. He stood quickly, backing up a few steps while trying to figure out what this new strangeness was.

It was lemmings. A lot of lemmings. They moved in unison with one another, small brown furry bodies packed together so tightly that they seemed to move as one being. They drifted quietly over to the heavy, flat stone that crushed his failed qalgi model. He could barely hear the sound of their tiny feet moving against the dusty soil. When they reached the stone, some of the lemmings nearest the rock began to dig, sending small puffs of dry soil floating through the air. Within minutes they had created tunnels under the stone. The boy sat in stunned silence, transfixed.

Lemmings would sometimes move in a mass if the area they inhabited became too populated and food sources became scarce. They would band together in a tight formation and strike out to find new territory. The sheer number of lemmings would ensure that at least some of them would survive if they ran into a predator. Piŋa had seen this happen a couple of times out on the tundra. But this seemed different to him. He sat still and watched, entranced by the display.

The lemmings crawled under the stone through the tunnels they had made, and within a few moments, the rock began shaking. Suddenly, they lifted it on their backs and moved the stone toward the boy. The stone looked like it was floating, with tens of tiny rodent feet underneath it, moving in slow, deliberate unison. When they got a few feet from the boy, the lemmings dug new tunnels, and the stone slowly lowered itself to its new spot. Then, one by one, the lemmings filed out from underneath the rock, leaving as quietly as they had come. The boy blinked in confusion at his lemming, staring at the creature in the silence left behind.

"What was that?" he asked, gesturing in the direction of

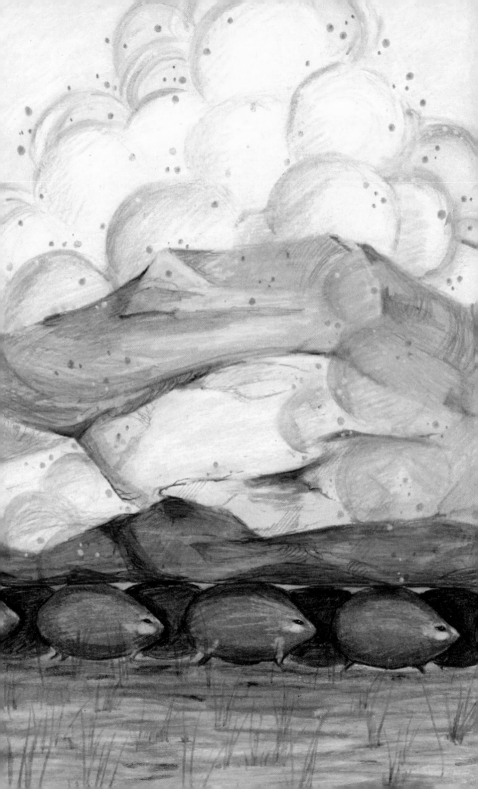

where the other lemmings had left. As an answer, the lemming squeaked and pointed its round rump at the boy, kicking its back feet and spraying dirt as it strode off.

The boy walked over to the stone and sat next to it. He lifted one side up, noting the softness of the disturbed soil underneath. *I guess if you live with eagle people, then odd lemmings are to be expected?* he wondered. Their behavior confused him, though.

What were they doing?

He examined the rock closer, noting again the heavy weight. It was amazing none of the lemmings had been crushed. The rock was easily twenty times their size. He had used rocks like these to build dead-fall traps for larger animals. The heaviness could have easily crushed one or two of them. Maybe even five of them. But they had been able to move it without hurting themselves.

How did *they move the rock?*

Each individual lemming was not very strong, but they combined their individual strength to accomplish something that seemed impossible.

All moving as one.

And then he realized that this was what they were trying to show him. The beams in a sod building were not strong enough to hold the weight of the sod by themselves, but they could hold a small part of the weight easily enough when combined with all of the other beams and poles and sod towers. The weight was being spread! Something small clicked in the boy's mind. Not much, but it was a start.

The boy bent over his model and began building it again. He could feel the resistance as he adjusted the pieces, and by the end of the day, he had a passable miniature section complete.

When the Eagle Mother came, Piŋa beamed and pointed his lips at his small accomplishment. "Lemming Hall," he said, and then laughed at his own joke. She snorted and then walked away, not even checking to see if he was following.

18

FIRST QALGI

The next few days, Piŋa practiced building the miniature qalgi. Savik met his newfound enthusiasm with suspicion at first, but didn't question it. Once the eagle man saw that the boy had mastered the small qalgi, he, Isiġnaq, and Piŋa packed some gear and made their way to the small valley the boy picked his greens in.

As they walked swiftly through the winding trail that crested the mountains, a large number of eagles flew above them, wings held wide to catch the rising mountain updrafts. Piŋa watched them all with curiosity. He had never seen so many of them alight before, and he was in awe at the sight.

Late summer was in full swing, and the sun beat down at

them with a dry, unrelenting heat magnified by the thin air. His skin prickled with sweat, and he was forced to stop and remove his thin summer parka. When they finally dropped into the small valley, he was relieved to find it somewhat cooler, the verdant plants and trickling creeks creating a pool of moisture in the air.

Even Savik seemed to relax a little once they arrived, forgoing the growls and scowls that were his usual self. They found a flat, open field that was mostly clear of brush and rocks, and made a temporary camp at the far end. That first day they mapped out the layout of the building, marking the entrances and approximate size with sticks jammed into the ground. The boy was immediately intimidated by the size. He imagined it was going to take him a long time to build this behemoth of a structure, even with Savik's help. It was not nearly as large as the eagles' hall, but it was still going to be the largest and most complicated thing he had ever built.

Later that night, the boy lay curled on the ground, wrapped in his sleeping skins, unable to sleep. This time of year, the sun hung low in the horizon, refusing to disappear. The lean-to they had built didn't block any of the light, and it intruded in his sleep no matter how he tucked himself under his skins. The tighter he wrapped himself up to block out the light, the hotter he got, and soon he was covered in sweat. He was so used to sleeping in the cool and dark eagles' hall. This open, wide space with unending sunlight grated at his mind like the nonstop trickling of the creek nearby . . . and that also would not let him rest. He knew in time exhaustion would give him no choice, but for now he was stuck listening to the thoughts in his head. Thoughts about home and his parents and his brothers. Thoughts about all the work he had to get done, a list that repeated itself over and over.

Annoyed that he wasn't going to get rest, the boy sat up and looked around. Surrounding him were eagles from the aerie, perched on logs and mounds of sod, all of them asleep. They varied in size and color. Some were almost as big as Savik in his eagle form, though a couple were much smaller. The smaller ones looked lighter in color, with white tufts of downy feathers showing at their breasts. There were at least twenty altogether that he could see. Savik and Isiġnaq also sat nearby in their human forms, quietly snoring in their sleep, faces slack and relaxed. He wondered why they were all there. It would only take one or two of them to keep him in check.

He reached over to his pack and pulled it toward himself, rummaging around to find the stash of dried fish that he had made from leftover meals the eagles had brought him. A few mosquitoes hovered around him, the high-pitched squeal of their wings drifting around his head. He swatted at the insects while the dried fish softened in his mouth.

He let his mind drift toward the Eagle Mother's words about this challenge being the end of his lessons. Tears wet his eyes as he thought about seeing his parents again. He tried not to think of them too much because it always left him weary and heartsore; instead he focused on the task he was given. But now, surrounded by sleeping eagles, his mind reached for them. He could almost hear his mother's nonstop talking, broken only by a warm smile. He could almost feel the pressure of his father's forehead on his own, his scent so like the ocean itself. Piŋa stared at the cleared field in front of him, and again he thought of the possibility of failure. What advice would they give him?

The sun had risen high, and even the insects were hiding from the midmorning heat. Luckily there was a breeze, so it wasn't completely unbearable, but even then, the boy decided to wear only a short pair of leather pants that he had made and some shin-high caribou-skin boots. The skin on his chest, arms, and back was pale compared to his hands and face, and he made a mental note to find some medicine and oil for the sunburn he knew would come later.

The other eagles had long since left Savik and the boy alone in the open field, and now the two of them worked at the ground with heavy pickaxes, digging down to make a large depression that would be about the same size as the finished qalgi, careful to preserve the squares of sod that they removed. The picks were not the most efficient at breaking through the loose stone and dirt, so the progress was slow.

They dug a tunnel at one end of the hall that would eventually become part of the entrance and would also work as a cold sink. A ditch ran the entire length and width of the entrance, to capture cold air and prevent it from pushing out the heat inside during the winter. It also served as a convenient place to store meat and keep it closer at hand during deep winter.

The boy had to rest often, as he got dizzy if he worked for too long. He had thought he was in good physical shape from all the dancing and his short hikes, but he realized quickly that he was far from fit. By midday his eyes drooped from lack of sleep. He didn't trust himself to swing the pickax, so he resigned himself to moving rocks by hand and clearing dirt to the sides. His arms burned with every stone, and his legs burned with every step. Soon his lower back went disturbingly numb, and his fingers found it hard to grip the rocks. He resorted to rolling the rocks slowly along the ground with the palms of his hands.

By late afternoon he finally reached his limit. Standing up slowly, he looked over the work he had done. It was a disappointing amount, barely any progress at all measured against the markers they had put into the soil. They hadn't even begun to gather materials to build the structure itself. That task alone would be monumental. He signaled to Savik that he was done. Without even waiting to see his response, Piŋa dragged his body to a shaded area under some scraggly willow brush. The soft moss gave way under his weight, and the cushioning provided him some relief. His eyes felt as if they were filled with grit and stung with every blink, so he closed his eyes for a moment.

He woke up a few hours later, coughing from a dry, parched throat. The coughing made his dry lips crack, and he tasted blood in his mouth. He tried to sit up and changed his mind when his muscles stiffened. Instead, he rolled over onto his back and stared at the cloudless sky. He waited for his sleep-heavy mind to catch up with the world. From the clearing, he heard shuffling noises, wings catching air, and mumbled curses. The dimming sun was blocked suddenly by Savik's shaggy-maned head. Dirt was smeared all over his face, making his deep scowl and disapproving face look comical. The boy smiled.

"Why are you smiling? And why are you napping? What do you need, boy?" he barked, as dust drifted down onto the boy's face. Piŋa chuckled, admiring the moment for its ridiculousness.

"This task is impossible, Savik. Look at me. I'm no match for the work. We won't be able to get this done before freeze-up. After it gets too cold, we won't be able to move anything at all. It's too much." Sighing, the boy rolled over again, this time doing it slowly and bracing himself for the pain. Piŋa sat up gingerly. "But some water would be a start." Savik sucked at his teeth and watched the boy.

"I'm out of shape, and I didn't sleep last night because of the sun," Piŋa said, gesturing at the sky with slow, stiff fingers. "I'll be fine once I start moving again." Savik grunted and tossed him a full leather bladder of water. The boy opened it and drank carefully. The sun-warmed water immediately soothed his dry mouth and lips.

"Don't push yourself too hard, boy. If you hurt yourself,

you won't be able to work for days. Better to go slow than to lose days or weeks due to injury."

"I don't want to go slow; I want to go home. I want to see my parents," Piŋa said under his breath, not looking at the man directly.

"We will get you home once you learn your last lessons, boy," Savik said just as quietly. "But you will do the work here first. What else do you need?"

Piŋa rolled his shoulders to loosen them up and then took another swig of the water. He frowned at Savik's question and scratched at the drying sweat and dirt in his hair with grimy fingernails. If only his frustration was so easily relieved as his itchy scalp.

"I would like ten of me to help build this qalgi. Maybe in better shape, though. Can you do that?" he said with impatience. "I am just a lowly weak human. I am trying my best. Unless you can give me some of that super eagle strength?"

Savik raised an eyebrow, a hint of a smile on his face. "Maybe," he said, and gestured vaguely above him. Piŋa was so consumed by his aches that the boy did not see at first what was happening. Two eagles slowly descended from the sky, carrying a log that was about two hands thick, their wingbeats timed perfectly with each other as they carefully dropped the log to the ground. The log sat next to other building materials that had not been there before: squares of sod in neat stacks, whale rib bones that gleamed pale, and a pile of driftwood logs in various sizes.

Savik noticed Piŋa staring as more eagles came. "Boy, you have to stop thinking of yourself as alone in your tasks. Why would you do things alone when you can accomplish so much more with help?" he said. "Sometimes all it takes is to say it. To say out loud what you need."

Piŋa became aware of an unfamiliar feeling as he took in what Savik was saying. He felt all at once grateful and indebted. He had never owed strangers anything before. With his family there was just *understanding*. The twofold feeling was something new and uncomfortable.

He noticed that Isiġnaq was sitting off to the side in her human form, picking dirt from under her nails with the sharp tip of her ulu. She occasionally shot angry looks in his direction. He smiled and waved at her and was met with a stony glance that was not the least amused.

He suddenly realized something about the other eagles. In the sunlight he could see that their coloring varied greatly, and some looked completely different than Savik's and Isiġnaq's eagle forms. Some were almost as dark as soot,

and a couple seemed to be a different type of eagle, with white heads and tail feathers. He turned to Savik.

"Are all these eagles your family? All of them?" he asked.

The man snorted at his question.

"No. A few are siblings; some are our young. The rest are the ones that occasionally live with us, who accept Mother as their leader. We work together on things, share food in exchange for cooperation."

The boy stared at the eagles. He had seen at least twenty that flew here with them, but there now seemed to be even more. So many. So many unrelated beings, and yet he had never seen fighting. Angry words, yes, but it never seemed to get further than that.

"How does Eagle Mother do it? Does she punish them? To make people live together and not be angry with one another?"

Savik chuckled under his breath and slapped his broad hand across the boy's back, making him wince in pain. "If that actually worked, we wouldn't need you, boy. Come. Do some of the stretches so we can at least clean up before we rest. Let's build you a better shelter to keep the sun from you so you can sleep."

The weeks passed by in a blur of physical labor, propelled by the boy's eagerness to finish. The work was hard on his body at first, but over time he was able to lift more, work longer. Blisters healed, and once pale skin browned in the sun. One of the sections of the qalgi collapsed twice, and it took Piŋa and Savik a week to figure out what they had done wrong. It took another week to tear down the section and rebuild it correctly.

But the day came when the building was completed, and it happened faster than the boy had ever thought possible. Every arch held true, every space was covered in sod, every piece of wood and bone braced skillfully to distribute the weight. The boy stood outside the building that they had raised from the soil. The sun sat behind him and lit the grand building in all of its glory and warmed his back. Savik walked up to stand beside him, his footsteps quiet as they both admired the building. They stood in silence for a time.

Twilight blanketed them as they packed their tools and got ready to sleep. The structure they had built was huge and eerily lifeless in the half-light. The absence of seal-oil lamps and people accentuated the emptiness. All of the eagles had gone, leaving just the boy and Savik behind. Piŋa stood at the entrance of the hall that he built, wondering what it would look like filled with people and not eagles. What would it sound like? What would his parents think of what he built? He yearned to be able to show them such a building, to hopefully build it *with* them one day.

19

EAGLE DRUM

He sat outside with the Eagle Mother and Savik, the wind blocked by the bulk of her great hall. It was nearly midday, and the sun was pinned in the sky high above them. The heat relaxed the boy as he repaired a hole in one of his boots with needle and thread. Savik and his mother had been sitting motionless for the whole morning, doing that weird eagle thing where they stared off into the distance and ignored him. Piŋa had brought his sewing kit, needing something physical to do, the nervous energy in him needing an escape.

When Eagle Mother finally spoke, her voice was subdued. "You have two more things to learn, boy. First, you will need to build another tool. The other, well, it is more of a frame of mind. I will begin with the one that you will find more difficult. You now know all that you need to hold a grand feast: You know about singing, dancing, and how to build a structure large enough to hold many people. Niqinaqi, boy. Do you know what it is to feast?"

The boy recalled all the lessons they had taught him. He thought of the drums and the songs, how they were not meant to be for just one person. He thought of the drummers and singers who taught him how to dance, of angry Alik and indifferent Pula. He thought of the qalgi and how many people it would be able to hold. He thought of his parents and brothers and their skills. He cleared his throat and stared at the dried grass in front of him. He plucked one and chewed on it, like his brother taught him to do. "We are to gather enough food to feed a hundred people, my family and I. And we are to hold a 'feast,' where we will sing and dance—and eat? Am I correct, Aana?"

A smile spread slowly across her face, and she leaned toward the boy. Her voice was a whisper. "Smart thoughts, boy, but what does all of this mean? For you?"

He frowned as he realized what she was getting at. "It means that we . . . I . . . will have to interact with other people. With strangers." He paused. "I can't control other people, Aana. They are afraid of us as much as we are afraid of them. I haven't even *seen* enough people in my lifetime to fill a qalgi. What you ask is . . . is going to be near impossible. Why would they listen to a boy like me? Where will I find them? What if they try to hurt me?" His voice trailed off.

She leaned back and gazed at the boy with golden, shimmering eyes, and he was reminded of who she was. Her next words were sharp and cut the air like talons slicing through soft meat. "You will do as I say, boy. This is the only reason we are returning you to your family. You will teach your parents what we have taught you. You will gather all the people, build the qalgi, and fill that qalgi with feasting and song and dance. You will hold it during early winter, after the freeze-up. The winter after next. This will give you more than enough time to prepare, to teach, to build."

She thought a moment. "But for the first feast, I shall give you some help. I know too well the separateness of the Iñupiaq people. So I shall tell you how to go about finding the people. Do you remember your brother's bow? The one with all the carvings of animal places on it?" Caught off guard, the boy could only nod. His mind scrambled to understand what the images of the animals and where to hunt them carved into the bow had to do with this mad task.

"When you are ready," the Eagle Mother continued, "you will visit all of those places. In each place you will meet people, who will always be in pairs. That is how you know they are for you. If you see more or fewer than two, you will not approach them. You will get rid of your fear of strangers." She eyed the boy. "Do you understand my instructions?"

The boy hid his doubts. He bowed his head and nodded his understanding.

"I also want you to create gifts for your guests, so they do not go home empty-handed. The world is a balance of energies. If you give without the expectation of receiving anything in return, this generosity will come back to you in the future."

He nodded. "Yes, Aana."

He heard the rustle of her garments as she moved. Her voice was quiet. "Boy, look at me." He tilted his head up so that she could see the lines of worry on his face. She examined him closely, but he could not tell by her expression what she found in him—or what she didn't find. "You won't know what I have given you yet. No. Not yet. But you look to have the stubbornness to do it. At least a little, ai? But you may also fail if you give in to your fear. Don't fail *me*, boy." Her golden eyes were subdued.

"Why, Aana? Why do I do all these things?" he asked.

"You will see why," she said as she pointed her stick at him. She placed a hand on Savik's shoulder to push herself up from the ground and slowly walked back to the entrance of her hall.

Savik rose up more swiftly than his mother. Piŋa glanced at his face and saw that there was genuine worry etched in Savik's brow. "What if I fail, Elder? Why is this so important?"

Savik kept his eyes on his mother's back. "You won't," he said. And he, too, strode off.

The boy hardly slept that night; even the cool and quiet of the eagles' hall didn't lull him to sleep like usual. He lay there in darkness listening to Eagle Mother's soft snoring, wondering when he would see his parents again. He had longed for the day that he would be able to return. It was the one goal that he had been marching toward since the beginning. The snoring intruded on his thoughts like waves, a rhythm of its own. He wondered what advice his father would give him now. He remembered watching his father repair a hole in his qayaq the day before he left for the mountains for obsidian. Piŋa had always been afraid of the ocean, afraid of the dark depths and powerful waves that tossed the slim boat about like it was a toy in a pond. But his father had never feared the waters. When he asked him why, his father always answered, "The waves are just waves; they are going somewhere. You can trust the waves to yearn for the land."

Trust the waves.

He slept so lightly that night that he woke up quickly when he heard Eagle Mother arise. He sat waiting for her when she came to collect him. She met his eagerness with raised eyebrows but said nothing. As they walked to the center of the hall, he could see a large, stout object hanging from the ceiling by a length of thick rope. Savik stood next to it, one hand holding it still so it did not swing about. Piŋa sat down across from Savik, awaiting instructions. Instead of speaking, the eagle man handed the object to the boy, indicating that he wanted him to examine it. Two sets of eyes watched the boy closely.

Piŋa stood and reached for it, and when Savik released

his grip, the boy realized why the rope was necessary. The object was heavy; without the rope it would be hard to hold for very long. It was rectangular in shape, and when he tilted it to look inside, he could see it was hollow, with open ends at the top and bottom like a tube.

Pictures of eagles in flight adorned the four sides of the rectangle. The images were expertly carved into the wood, and the birds seemed to move as he turned it around. The rope that held the box was attached at the top so that it hung like an elaborate pillar. When he was done with his examination, Piŋa glanced up expectantly at the two eagles. Savik reached behind him and produced a carved wooden stick; it was short, only about the length of his forearm, and heavier at one end. He handed this to the boy.

Puzzled, the boy took the stick and stared at it. It reminded him of the sticks they used for drumming. He held it by the slimmer end in his right hand and then balanced the box in his left. With a glance at the eagles, who watched him silently, he carefully struck the hovering box with the stick.

The sound made the hair on his arms stand up. He knew that sound. It was a sound that he had lived with for over a year, the same sound he'd first heard on his journey up the

mountains with Savik. He had gotten so used to hearing it daily that the fact that he could reproduce the sound startled him. It was the sound of the Eagle Mother's heartbeat. He glanced at her and found her smiling, her eyes shimmering in the half-light.

"I will be there with you," she said in a clear voice. "I will be present at all feasts that you and your people hold. This drum can only be used when you sing certain songs. And when you strike it, all will feel my presence. I will preside always over the gift that I have given you." She arose in one fluid motion and walked to her pile of furs, where she lay down and closed her eyes.

Savik stood next to the boy. He handed him a length of hardwood. He moved the eagle drum from the boy's hand and held it out of his reach.

"You will not strike the drum again, not here, anyway. To learn these songs, you will strike this piece of wood instead."

"Why? Why this drum and not the others?"

"Why do you think, boy? This drum is made to draw us to you, to connect us," Savik responded quickly, gesturing in the direction of his mother. The boy imagined it worked like some sort of signal.

He thought about Eagle Mother's twisted stick and the markers along it. About her warnings about ending up one of those strings. Why would they trust him even with this bit of power? What if he messed it all up somehow?

Trust the waves. All waves turned toward the shore. The eagles wanted him to succeed, to create this bond for them. He had to keep that in mind.

20

HOME

The boy was wrong in one thing. It took him only one turn of the moon to learn the last of his lessons. By then the world was deep into falltime. The air was heavy with cold moisture, the green was replaced with more earthen colors, and frost crept from the deepest parts of the earth late at night and disappeared by morning. Once again the caribou bulls lost all of their fat, but this time the eagles knew not to hunt the animals that were in rut. Most of that time, Pina studied how the special drum was built. Just like with the other drums, he was told to build it by replicating the original. The large planes of wood were hard to come by in the treeless expanses of the Arctic tundra, so the eagles once again brought him sections of driftwood from a faraway shore. He took care to shave them carefully with a sharp adze to match the thickness and size of the original drum. He also learned and memorized the songs that would honor Eagle Mother and her brood, songs that spoke of their powerful presence.

He knew the day when he would be allowed to leave would come soon, but he was afraid to ask, afraid they would refuse him again and invent some strange new task for him. So he waited.

The day came sooner than he'd thought.

He awoke to a commotion in the hall. Slowly, in a sleepy daze, he looked around. There were several figures moving around, collecting objects from the ground and shelves. Curious, the boy stored his sleeping furs and dressed himself quickly.

Savik stood in the middle of the hall with the boy's pack slung over his shoulder. The pack looked repaired, and it bulged with its contents. In his other hand, Savik held the boy's bow. The sinew had been replaced once again, bending it into a graceful curve. For once, Savik greeted the boy with a pure smile, without the usual grimace. He waved the bow in the boy's direction.

The boy ran up to Savik, almost afraid to ask. But he asked anyway. "Am I going home, Elder?"

Savik raised an eyebrow at the boy's use of *Elder* instead of his name. He turned and took long strides to the entrance of the hall, calling over his shoulder, "Well, you cannot stay here forever."

The boy hurried after the eagle, a cautious elation coursing through his body. When he followed Savik outside into the crisp morning air, he paused and looked back at the grand qalgi that had been his home for almost a year and a half. He looked around for the Eagle Mother, but she was nowhere to be seen.

Savik glanced back and saw the boy hesitating at the entrance. His voice was soft but clear. "She does not say goodbye, boy."

Piŋa nodded.

"Besides, she will always be with you."

The boy understood. The two of them gazed over the edge of the mountain. His excitement dimmed as he realized that the journey back would be a long one and that he wouldn't see his parents for a time yet.

Savik pushed the pack into Piŋa's hands and examined the boy closely. "Are you brave, boy? Do you want to see your parents as soon as possible?"

At his words, Piŋa's throat tightened. He nodded and squared his shoulders as he slung the pack over a shoulder, hoping that he looked braver than he felt.

Savik stared into his eyes for a long time. Finally, he nodded. He turned his back to the boy and motioned him closer. Piŋa moved toward him and paused, not sure what was being asked of him. Savik crouched a little lower, tilting his back so it was more horizontal. It took a moment to realize what the eagle was asking him to do. He moved closer to the man and took a deep steadying breath, trying to calm the tremble in his hands. The boy pulled himself onto the broad, slippery, feathered back of Savik's parka and wrapped his arms tightly around the sinewy neck. He was amazed to find that his weight did not impede Savik's movement at all as he walked to the edge of the precipice.

Savik turned his head and gave the boy the last instructions he would ever give him. "Remember what we have taught you, and remember what you have to do. You have two winters to complete it. We will be watching you closely." Savik reached a hand up and carefully lifted the hood of his feather parka over his head. "And hang on tight. It would be a shame to lose you now."

When the great eagle's parka hood covered the man's face, the boy felt the body beneath him shift. Suddenly afraid, Piŋa closed his eyes, not wanting to see the change Savik was undergoing. He felt the great eagle body shiver for a moment as the transformation ended. He kept his eyes closed as Savik crouched low and then leapt from the mountaintop. He felt the world drop, felt a screaming wind tear at his face. His stomach lurched, and he was suddenly glad that he had not eaten that morning.

The flight down was just as silent as the journey up the mountain had been. All the boy could hear was the rush of wind streaming past his face. His hair whipped about, stinging his face where it lashed his cold skin. Not once did he feel the great eagle flap his wings. All he could feel was the minute adjustments that the bird made as the currents buffeted them from all directions. Hot tears leaked from his eyes and burned trails on his brow and up into his scalp. It was not just the wind that made those tears.

They flew for hours, and never once did his grip on Savik's neck loosen. He saw flashes of color behind his eyelids from holding them shut tight for so long. He got the courage to open his eyes once and was met with such a sudden wave of vertigo that it made him afraid to open them again. That small glimpse showed the world distant and tiny beneath them, with nothing but never-ending open sky above them. When his belly started to growl and his bladder became a hard rock in his gut, he did not let the eagle know. He did not want to postpone meeting his parents any more than he already had.

He knew they were growing closer to his home when he felt the air begin to warm around his body. Then the eagle began to slow their descent. The powerful wings captured the air around them, the force pushing the boy deeper into the eagle's back. The boy opened his eyes at the last moment, just in time to see the ground rushing toward them, a brown blur that leapt up to catch them. They landed haphazardly, and the boy was flung forward. He tumbled over the bird's head and landed on his back. Luckily, the tundra was soft and eased the impact, but he was still left breathless.

Piŋa lay there gathering himself, transfixed at the eagle, who was panting with the exertion from the flight.

Savik's great golden feathers were ruffled, and he preened and smoothed them with his beak. For some reason, this made the boy laugh. He laughed so hard his sides ached, and tears ran down his face. The eagle impassively watched the boy, first with one eye, then with the other. When the laughing fit was finally over, the boy rose to his feet and, still smiling, nodded his head in the eagle's direction. Still chuckling, he turned away and relieved himself before the laughing did it for him. He realized then that he was happy, the feeling rolling over him like a warm bearskin blanket. He was going home.

Home.

Savik pulled his wings close to his body, then spread them, and with a great deal of flapping and a lucky wind, climbed into the air. With a hand on his brow, the boy watched him, still amazed at the sight of this great beast he had come to know. The eagle circled twice, letting out a series of cries, before taking off toward the mountains. Piŋa frowned, sure he was being told off again. The eagle never once looked back.

Alone, the boy took stock of where he was, looking for familiar landmarks and direction markers. After a few moments, he realized that he was only an hour or so from his parents' sod house. With renewed energy, he struck off into the tundra. His pack seemed light, and his step became almost a dance as he skipped across the sweet-scented grass. He began to sing as he went, timing the song to his steps. He sang of lichen and aqpik berries, of duck hunting and the scent of seal oil. He sang of a mother's love and a father's pride. He sang of lost brothers and copper-tipped eagle feathers. He sang of his return home.

21

REUNION

Fourteen moons after the day they last saw their son, they heard the boy's singing first. They understood the words but were mystified by the rhythmical yelling. His mother swore that it was some sort of spirit and ordered Father to get his spears. And that was how they greeted him—Mother hiding behind Father, who held a spear at the ready, while the boy, dressed in unadorned furs, hurried across the tundra toward them.

"Aakaaŋ! Aapaaŋ!" the boy yelled as soon as he saw them. Father's spear and pack were both instantly forgotten and fell to the ground. Piŋa ran to them, arms outspread.

"Iġñiin! Son!" his mother called back. Her hands found

themselves on the sides of his face, brushing his hair from his eyes. "You are *back*. You are really *back*." Tears fell from her in rivers. She touched his face over and over, as she reassured herself that he was real. Father fell to his knees in front of them both, laughing with great joy, letting out great bellowing *"Ui! Ui!"* at seeing his family reunited. Every once in a while, Father reached out and hugged the boy, arms encompassing his wife as well, to make sure his son was real and alive and back again, a happy grin on his normally serious face.

"How?" Father asked. "How did you find your way back? And what happened? We thought we lost you, son."

"A long story! All I could think of was to return to you both. I missed you."

It was a reunion that held immeasurable joy, for they had given up on ever finding their youngest son, just as they had given up on their other sons.

They spent long moments watching one another in the setting tundra sun. The boy noted the deeper lines on their faces and the presence of more gray in their hair, and they noticed how tall he had become, how he seemed graceful and strong, no longer gangly. They laughed at things that weren't really funny and touched one another's arms, a hand or a cheek, simply to know that the other existed. Later that evening, when all was quiet, they sat around the fire, and he began to tell them how he met Savik and where he had gone.

For the next turning of the moon as the world gave way to winter, they simply enjoyed being a family again. Eventually, the boy told them all the details of his journey and of the tasks the eagles had given him. He told them of the qalgi in the sky and the graceful eagle women who sang notes of golden sunshine. And with an aching heart, he told them of the gruff Savik, who had killed his older brothers without hesitation, news that gave them peace in a way and made room for the pain to be put to rest. He talked of the old Eagle Mother, whose heartbeat could be felt for miles. He told his parents all that he had learned and all that he had built in that magnificent place that humans had never known. He told them also of the great burden that the eagles had placed on his shoulders, what they expected of him and his parents.

"And what if we fail?" his father asked. "What if you do all they ask of you and still fail because no one comes? What then?"

"They said I would be punished. Like my brothers," Piŋa said quietly. Father's face hardened. He reached into his parka and brought out the tiny ivory goose that looked even more worn down than he remembered. He placed the charm in Piŋa's hands, closing the boy's fingers tightly around it.

"Then we will not fail. We will not fail in this," he said.

Piŋa touched foreheads with his father, willing with all of his determination for it to be a truth. At least he would not be alone in his work.

They planned the next year carefully. The amount of work was enormous, and a lot of it was unfamiliar. They concentrated on tackling it all step by step.

First, they needed to increase the food they harvested. This meant more time to hunt and more space to store it all.

Second, they had to start preparing now. When the season turned completely and winter arrived in force, they turned their attention to the gifts. His mother, surprised and excited by her son's request, began making beautiful mittens and pouches. With skillful hands, she created all manner of things from bits of fur, bone, beads, and ivory—little things that could be easily carried home. His father went to the ocean more often and came back with shimmering seal hides and opalescent polar bear hides. The boy extended his trapline and brought home furs that were thick and glistening.

When spring arrived, they built three more underground

storage mounds to hold the meat they would need. The boy returned to the mountains, making several trips to gather obsidian and slate that he and his father used to made razor-sharp spear tips, arrowheads, ulus, and knives.

In the summer and fall, they harvested caribou and fish, and his mother gathered berries and herbs from the tundra. They dried and smoked and preserved everything they could. During that time, the boy built many drums with his parents, including the special eagle drum that mimicked the Eagle Mother's heartbeat. He took care to show them the best ways to harvest and treat the wood and how to prepare the delicate skins needed for the drum coverings.

In the evenings, when the world was quiet, they would sit around the cooking fire, and the boy would teach his parents the songs he knew and how to use their voices to evoke emotion. They would take turns between drumming and singing and learning the motions to the dances. Surprisingly, his father possessed a loud and exceptional singing voice, and his mother's voice was clear and precise. Both were talented and enthusiastic dancers. He was amazed to see how quickly they learned. Amazed, too, that they were even better song makers than he, for they had much more experience in this world.

They also created songs together as a family. One song was about the moment they saw one another on that tundra slope when he returned to them, and the joy and celebration that came afterward. They laughed at the part of the dance where Father held a spear in the air, and how Mother thought he might be a spirit.

And when the larders were full and the house brimmed with goods, and the spring thawed the ground, the boy and his father and mother began the task of building the qalgi.

They chose a level site near their home, making sure that the area was sound and would not be flooded with the changes in the seasons. The day was bright and clear and still a little chilly from the leftovers of winter. The boy measured off the size of the building, taking care to mark it with sticks hammered into the soil. His father frowned from off to the side.

"Are you sure you need such a large building? It's probably going to collapse in on itself," he said. The boy smiled at his father's comment, remembering a time where he had thought the same thing.

"It will work, Aapa. Look, I will show you." He cleared a space on the ground and sharpened a stick to draw with. He drew a cross section of the qalgi. "See here? The weight coming from the top has to be spread so that it is smaller and then matched by the weight of the walls. So if you want a bigger space, then you must add more here and here." He pointed his stick at the sidewalls and the beams. "And we will add a few internal posts, but that is more to account for shifting."

His father grunted. "I never thought you had a mind for this type of thing, son. You never seemed interested in it much."

The boy smiled. "A lemming taught me how to build."

"I don't like lemmings; they get into all your food in the house!" his mother said as she joined them on the construction site. She looked around at the markers on the ground. "This building is too big, son; how are we going to build such a thing?"

"Well, we should probably start with gathering the materials. Then we can focus on building?" His parents agreed with his suggestion.

The spring storms had washed up massive logs and bones onto the beach, and it made it easy pickings for the family. They started there first, dragging back the beams to the construction site with the help of the dogs. They took time then to shape some of the wood. His mother enjoyed this part, so they let her do most of the work. Her hands moved across the wood just as they did when she worked on skins, and the beams were smoother and more consistent in thickness than anything the boy and his father could do.

Next they focused on gathering all the sod. They had purposefully chosen a site that was near a river. They used the river to haul the sod from inland, where it grew thicker and was easier to harvest. They would have the dogs pull the empty boat upriver against the current, running along each bank, guided on each side by the boy and his father, while Mother sat in the boat and steered with the oars. They would then fill the boat with as much sod as they could and float it back toward the ocean to the qalgi, while the dogs happily ran back along the banks chasing squirrels.

With all three working toward their goal, the gathering of materials went quickly, and soon they began building the qalgi itself. They started with digging into the earth to lower the floor of the building, and then they dug the tunnel that would serve as the main entrance. This part went quicker than it did for the boy and the eagles, as the soil here was deeper and looser along the coast. The internal beams went up next, and then sod was stacked on the side to brace the beams for the weight of the roof.

The boy told his parents about the little lemming he had befriended as they worked, and how the lemming had helped him understand how a qalgi could withstand a great weight. He told them of how the knowledge his mother had given him about plants had helped him with that friendship and had kept him healthy during his stay there. Her smile at these stories brightened. And when she looked at him, he felt she truly saw him, and only him. They worked hard, and soon enough the qalgi was finished, a lot quicker than the boy thought possible.

His parents marveled at its mammoth size, and they wondered where the boy would find enough people to fill it. They worried about him meeting strangers, and though they never brought up their own experiences of when they were young, Piŋa could see the fear in their eyes. He had left them before, and they had thought they lost him for good. He assured them as best as he could, taking his time to pack all of the things they suggested, repeating all the advice that they gave him, so that they knew he was listening to them. He promised that if things got bad, he would not pursue the people. But he had to try and follow the Eagle Mother's directions.

When all was ready, the boy took up his bow and gear,

briefly touched foreheads with his parents, and started walking to the places that his second brother had etched into the
length of the bow. He told his parents to start expecting
people in three turnings of the moon, and then set off, with
trepidation, to complete the last part of his journey.

22

FINDING STRANGERS

Fall was arriving again when he set out to find the people who would fill the giant qalgi. The air was becoming cool at night, and the sun was dipping lower in the sky, letting nighttime grow a little longer each day.

Following the eagles' instructions, the boy examined the etchings on his bow. Most of the images were faded, but he knew them all by heart. He touched the image of the ptarmigan perched in the willow tops in spring, remembering the time his brothers had showed him how to trap them with snares. Each carving was attached to a memory, some good and some full of failure. But the love he had for his brothers was present in every single one. He decided to start with the farthest from his home and work his way back.

He journeyed first toward the place where his brother had etched geese preening in water. On his way, he relied on roots and berries and leaves he could find as he walked, and a hefty bag of dried meat he carried to feed himself. He didn't have much time to spare and so didn't take the time to hunt as he went. His destination was a marshy land carpeted with orange aqpik berries and dotted with giant lakes of clear water. He made camp in the lee of a small hill and waited, not knowing what to expect. The calls of migrating birds filled the air day and night. This world smelled of stagnant water and sweet grass. Insects of every kind worked frantically in the air, taking advantage of the animals that were preoccupied, a constant background noise of wings.

He found them when the sun was at its lowest and the sky was sooty. From his hill, he spotted the warm glow of a campfire in the distance. He was afraid at first and began packing his gear, instinct telling him he must avoid contact. Then he remembered those piercing golden eyes and the command that Eagle Mother had given him. With dread, he gathered his gear and began to pick his way toward the flickering campfire in the distance.

When he was close enough, he made out two figures lounging near the fire, one smaller than the other. Cautiously, Piŋa slowed his steps and, with fluid movements, unstrung his bow and strapped it to his back. Then he took his knife and tucked it deep into the folds of his parka so it was not visible. He approached the fire with empty hands, making sure that they could hear him coming by making his steps louder than normal in the crunchy grass. Both figures stood up slowly as he made his way leisurely toward them. When he was close enough, he called out to them. "Greetings!" he shouted, trying to sound friendly and unconcerned. "I come with news!"

They met his announcement with stony silence.

As he got closer, he realized that the smaller figure was a child, a boy by the look of his parka, barely old enough to start using a man's bow. The other was a man about the same age as his father. Both wore clothing made of goose feathers, finely stitched and pristine. He could see no weapons of any kind nearby, and indeed he did not even see any packs they might have carried. They watched him with bright round eyes.

Piŋa stopped at the edge of the firelight, where they could see him clearly. The older man smiled and showed him his bare, calloused hands. His voice was loud, and he spoke in an odd way, almost as if he could pronounce only one word in each breath. "Come, stranger," he said, "and tell us your news." He waved for Piŋa to sit near the fire. The boy sat where he'd been directed and made sure his hands stayed in clear view.

When he was settled, the child reached behind and pulled from the grass a platter that steamed in the air. With a stilted walk and barely contained shyness, the child placed the platter in front of the boy. When he looked down, the boy realized that the platter was heaped with roasted fish, and his stomach grumbled. He didn't expect such a response. He expected to be questioned right away. Somehow the presence of the food and their generosity made him feel more at ease. Nodding his thanks and making sure to smile, he reached down and began to eat. The man and child waited, amused at the boy's obvious hunger.

When Piŋa finished eating, he placed the platter on the ground in front of him and cleared his throat. "Thank you for your kindness," he said. "I come with news that my family will be holding a feast this winter, three turns of the moon from now. You and your son are invited to join us. Stories will be told, gifts will be given, and you will be fed well."

The man nodded and asked for directions to where the gathering was going to be held. Carefully the boy leaned over and, with the tip of his bow, drew a map on the ground showing where they had placed the qalgi. It was how his father, mother, and brothers shared information—where they were headed, where they had seen something interesting, and the like. It worked well for this purpose. When the man seemed to understand the directions, the boy leaned back and strapped his bow back onto his pack.

"We will be happy to attend," the man said, nodding to his child. "We will be there with some of our family who have decided to remain longer in this area. Please, stay the night and share our camp and fire." With that, the father and son settled down on mats of woven grass and soon were fast asleep.

The boy suddenly realized that he was very tired. The warm food combined with the stress of the meeting made him yawn. He quietly took out his sleeping mat and laid it out at the edge of the fire's light, grateful for its warmth. He lay down, and in no time, he was asleep.

When he awoke the next morning, he was alone. The fire had been carefully banked so that it still radiated heat. All that was left were the bones from the fish he had eaten the

night before. There were no signs—not even footprints—
that the man and his son had ever been there. Though the boy
found this very odd, he still had to trust the Eagle Mother's
orders, and so he did not dwell long on the strangeness. With
renewed determination and pleasure at his first success, he
started hiking to the next place on his bow.

The area he was headed to was where three major valleys
met. Here, two rivers merged and continued north to the
ocean. The valleys created a Y shape that spanned at least
three days' walk across. It was a very animal-rich area, both
predator and prey, and he was not surprised that the bow
told of three separate places here that he was supposed to
encounter people for the feast.

The first area was dense willow brush, unusual in that
they were some of the tallest he had ever seen. The trunks
were almost as thick as his waist, and they towered over
him, blocking out the sun as they tangled with one another,
fighting for sunlight. He could not see very far in the dim
light, and it made him nervous. He slowly worked his way
through the odd forest, following the winding river, hoping
he would see the people he had to meet before he ran into
a bear. He found a low hill, climbed to its top, and waited
for the darkness so that he could hopefully see a firelight.

He did not know how he was supposed to find these people otherwise.

A few hours later, he spotted a flickering light through the dense brush, a faint glow he could barely see. He made his way slowly through the darkness. When he got close enough that he knew they could hear him, he made sure to make his footsteps loud enough that he wouldn't startle them too much. When he reached the fire, he was surprised to see no one there. He called out into the darkness, hoping that they were nearby. When he didn't get a response, he sat down by the fire and waited. Was he in the wrong area? Did they leave? The fire was freshly tended, so he knew they weren't far if they did leave.

Just when he started wondering what he should do next, he heard a faint scuffing of the dirt behind him. He turned slowly and smiled at the darkness, his hands out in front of him to show he had no weapons.

"Hello! I am looking for a pair of people. I bring news! Sorry to startle you; I mean no harm."

Two short and fairly plump people emerged slowly from the darkness toward the fire. When they came into the firelight, he could see that both were women from the long parkas they wore made from thick rabbit skins. They stopped at the edge of the light, clasping each other's hands and leaning forward to get a look at his face. They seemed to both have bad eyesight. Heavy, thick braided hair framed round, dark faces.

"What do you want with us?" the older woman asked.

"I only wish to tell you news, to tell you about the feast and gathering my family is holding this winter. I am inviting those that might want to attend."

"Why would we come to your gathering? Is it some sort of trick? Do you have proof?" The woman fired the questions at him, while her smaller companion nodded her head.

"I . . . well. Proof? I don't know what the proof would be. We will be providing food for our guests, there will be dancing, and singing, and we are offering our hospitality to any who come." He stumbled through the sentence. "Will you at least let me draw you a map to show you where it will be? It is no trick." He could feel the nervousness from the women, and it made him nervous, too. But he had a task to complete. "And then I will leave."

The women whispered to each other and then nodded at the boy. They slowly approached him and watched from a distance as he cleared an area and drew the map showing where the qalgi was. When he was done, he assured them

again that he hoped they would attend, but they would only respond with a quiet "Maybe, maybe." He left as soon as he could, not wanting to worry them any more than he had to.

That night he walked a good distance from their fire and found a small hill to sleep next to. He would be paranoid, too, if he had to live in that dense brush. With their bad eyesight, they probably couldn't see very far around them. He hoped the women would come. What if they didn't? What would the Eagle Mother do if no one showed up? His stomach ached the more he thought about it, and he had to stop and drink his fill of water till the pain went away.

The next spot was in the other end of the Y of the valleys. It was a valley filled with trickling creeks beside a wide, shallow river, and deep pools of moving water filled with dense, water-loving plants. Different types of willow brush grew here, though they were of the normal-size variety. This time he didn't see a fire when he found the people.

He was making his way down the edge of an especially deep creek, when suddenly something heavy hit him in the back of the head, knocking him to the ground.

23

LAST STOP

He rolled his body as soon as he realized what had happened. He came up on his feet and reached for his knife. But he forgot his knife was tucked deep inside his parka, so he squared off, his hands up to protect his face, and turned toward whatever had slapped him.

An incredibly tall man emerged from the brush, his heavy, bushy brows almost covering his eyes completely as he frowned at the boy. A slightly smaller figure stood behind him in the brush. The man stepped closer to the boy, his arms raised in a threatening manner.

"Who are you? And what are you doing in our territory?" the man bellowed at the boy.

"I'm just a messenger! Piŋa is my name. I am here looking for people to invite to a gathering!" the boy sputtered out quickly.

"Oh," the man said simply. His demeanor changed as he looked the boy over and saw that he held no weapons. The boy could see the man was dressed in nothing but thick, dark leather from head to toe. "Sorry about knocking you down; can't be too careful around here." Piŋa quickly nodded. He stood up and carefully brushed some of the dirt from his clothes.

"My fault, too; I wasn't really paying attention where I was headed," the boy replied. "Like I said, I am delivering a message. Me and my family are holding a big feast at our new qalgi. We will be providing food for anyone that shows up. There will be dancing and singing and many stories, I'm sure. You and your family are invited."

The man turned to the figure in the willows and gestured for the other person to come out. It was a young woman, who was almost as tall as the man. The boy had never seen such a tall woman before. She blushed a deep red and made her way slowly toward them.

"This is my daughter. We are camping with our family farther down this valley. We will talk to the rest of our family about going to your gathering. When and where is it?"

The boy smoothed out the sand and drew a map. When the father seemed to understand where it was, the boy stood up and decided that since there was light left, he was going to find a place to camp. They parted on good terms, and the boy made his way toward the last arm of the Y-shaped valley. It would take him longer to get there, so he continued to walk until darkness forced him to make a quick camp in the lee of a rocky ledge.

A day and a half later, he arrived at the area he was looking for. The terrain was flat and wide, with very little brush or vegetation, and hundreds of rocky outcrops that made perfect places for marmot and squirrels to build their homes. In the winter, this part of the valley became deep with snow, and the heavy river that wound lazily through the valley froze into a perfect path for animals to move quickly over. The river itself cut into the earth and created sheer, jagged cliffs that rose high and dark against the sky, giving the area a foreboding feel. It perfectly mirrored the carving on the boy's bow—a wolf standing in front of a frozen river with sheer cliffs on either side.

The boy had dropped down into the valley and found a sandbar to make a temporary camp. He was trying to figure out how to find the people he was looking for. The images on his bow didn't give specific places, just general areas. The cliffs were just a landmark. He decided to take the rest of the day and make himself a hot meal. It had been a while since he had one.

He walked along the river till he found what he was looking for: an area where the river split into slower-moving and shallower waters. He could see the flash of fish tails in the deeper parts as grayling jumped to the surface to eat insects. He took a length of sinew and attached a fishhook that he had made from ivory and cast it into the water. Almost immediately the fish bit his hook, and he pulled them one by one to shore. He gathered some dried wood and built himself a fire on the sandbar, excited to eat a fresh, hot meal. He tossed some fresh sargiq leaves into the fire, too, to deter the mosquitoes that had found him, and he speared a fish with a stick of green willow.

He was spinning the stick over the fire when he heard footsteps behind him in the dark. He jumped up and turned, squinting into the darkness as he slowly reached for his bow and arrows. He could make out two tall, dark figures making their way toward him from the far side of the sandbar. When they got close enough for him to see them in the firelight, he was surprised that he recognized one of them.

"Alik," the boy said.

The man in the black wolf parka came out of the dark, that eerie bright smile on his face. He looked exactly the same as the boy remembered him from their time with the eagles. Next to him stood another man, who was a good head taller than Alik. This strange man wore a parka made from gray wolf skins; his face was long and pointed, and his shoulder-length, thick hair added to his intimidating appearance.

The man chuckled and smiled at Alik. "That is a funny name to pick for yourself."

Alik shrugged and looked away. Clearly this other man in the gray parka was in charge. Piŋa stood up slowly and smiled a little.

"I am a messenger. I bring news of a feast and a gathering that my family—"

"Yeah, we know. We heard you talking to that tall man. And we have been watching you for a while." The man walked over to the fish and picked it out of the coals, eyeing the boy to see what he would do. "We agreed to meet you, but I don't think any of our kind will attend." He took a careful bite of the steaming fish, not even bothering to remove the prickly fins.

The boy's heart sank a little. He tried again.

"We don't require anything from our guests in return. We only wish to gather together and share stories. And eat good food. Your family would be welcomed, and if you have any concerns, I can try and address those."

The man tossed the rest of the fish down next to the fire and turned his attention to the boy.

"We just don't like you, is all. None of our family will attend. In fact, you should probably leave this valley tonight."

The boy's eyes widened. "Tonight?" he asked.

"Yes, tonight," the man said as he kicked sand over Piŋa's campsite, ruining the rest of the fish and effectively smothering his fire.

The boy blinked a few times, unsure of what he had done to get such a reaction, but he started packing his gear. When he looked up, the man in the gray wolf parka was walking back into the darkness. Alik still stood near him, though. He stared at the boy.

"I don't understand, but I will leave tonight," Piŋa told Alik. "I don't want trouble."

Alik crossed his arms. His normally scowling face was contemplative.

"I'll pass along your message to the other family members, because I know your task was set by the eagles. But don't expect any of them to be there."

The boy nodded, knowing this was the best he could ask for. How was he supposed to argue? What could he say? Did Alik's family treat everyone like this?

He trudged into the night, his ears perking up at any sound that he heard behind him, but no one followed him out of the valley.

The rest of the meetings went along the same lines. Sometimes the people would greet him with kindness, sometimes they gave him a "maybe," and sometimes they met him with hostility or indifference or fear. Whenever he could, he would at least draw the map for them and encourage them to invite others, but as the meetings went on, he could not say how many people—if any at all—were coming.

He had only one place left to visit before it was time to head back home for the feast. Winter had arrived, and the ground was now laden with thick snow, so traveling became a constant battle between him and the elements. His tall winter boots were wet from dragging them through the snow, and he was slowed down significantly. He stopped for a few days and made himself a pair of snowshoes from the twisted branches of willow and some sinew that he carried in his pack.

The last spot was closest to his home. He would look for the final pair beside the river that ran alongside his newly constructed qalgi. Glad that his duty was almost at an end, he quickened his pace despite the snow. He was moving so quickly that he almost missed the glow of their fire.

The fire was set deep in the willows in a hollow dug out in the snow. Two round men sat relaxing in its glow. The boy approached them as he had all the others, with empty hands and slow steps. They greeted him warmly and offered him a place next to their fire. When he was settled and had finished explaining why he was seeking them out, they gave him a large bowl filled to the brim with steaming fish soup. He murmured his thanks as he drained the bowl of its warm contents. The round men were greatly amused, and it was a pleasant surprise to the boy. They wore beaver skins, and the boy was in awe of the quality of the hides, for they glowed a deep amber color in the firelight. When he finished eating, he set down the bowl and leaned back, enjoying the warmth from the fire and the soup.

Look at me, relaxing with strangers. Who would have thought this was possible? he thought to himself.

"So tell us where the feast is going to be held, young boy, so that we may join you." The man's voice was high-pitched, and he made an odd chirping noise in the back of his throat as he spoke.

"I am headed back there," the boy said. "We can travel together if you wish."

Both men nodded in unison, smiles lighting their faces. The boy could see that they had protruding front teeth, which gave them both a slightly comical look.

"It will be a pleasure, young one. We will sleep and then head out tomorrow, ai?" And both men curled into hollows they'd made in the snow and fell asleep, snoring loudly. The boy again took out his sleeping gear—which would need to be replaced soon—and dug himself a place to sleep in the soft snow. He, too, fell asleep quickly.

In the morning, the boy awoke to the sound of the men chuckling as they banked the fire. He got up quickly and gathered his gear, not wanting to be the slow one of the group. When he was finished, they all set out down the river to their final destination. He found the two men to be pleasant traveling company. They told jokes and laughed frequently, flashing their bright front teeth. As they walked, the two men would stop frequently and strip the outer bark from willow branches. They chewed on the pieces. He thought it odd but figured that it might be some sort of medicine. His mother taught him about how to use the willow bark for pain relief, but he thought it would be rude to ask a stranger about such an odd habit.

The boy marveled at how much his life had changed. Here he was traveling with strangers, on their way to hopefully meet up with even more strangers.

Soon enough, the boy smelled the heavy scent of a cooking fire on the wind; the sharp tang of burning willow wood and steam mixed in the most pleasant way with the smell of cooking fat and frying meat. It made his mouth water at the thought of the food that awaited ahead. He knew he was close to home.

The sound of the two men chatting was drowned out by the worry that suddenly rose up inside of him. What if he failed? What if the people did not come as they said they would? Would Eagle Mother and her brood come to exact revenge on him and his family?

Don't get ahead of yourself, Piŋa, he thought to himself, but it wasn't very comforting.

He walked faster, leaving the two men behind, wanting to see what lay ahead of him.

24

QALGI

When he crested the last small hill and spotted the qalgi, the boy was surprised to see that the long building was completely surrounded by camps. He was surprised, too, to see that most of the people he'd invited—and some who were complete strangers—were there sitting around small fires. Relief washed over him as he looked at all of the people. Most of the guests recognized him and called out warm greetings from where they sat. The boy smiled and waved at them, hesitantly and awkwardly at first, but with more energy as he made his way through. He had never seen so many people in one place, and even though it made him a little uneasy, he was also excited. *What stories do they have to tell us? What adventures and knowledge?*

He helped the two round men he was traveling with find a good place to set up their camp and went to look for his parents. When he reached his sod house, his parents were not there. He stored his gear and ventured back out. He found his mother at a camp with several people dressed in owl feather clothing. She sat talking with an older lady, her face flushed with excitement. When he got close, they both greeted him with smiles and waved for him to sit.

"This woman is telling me about the antics of her sons," his mother said. "You are so much like her sons. It's amazing." She turned back to the woman, and they both laughed, their eyes bright with amusement.

Smiling, the boy got up and looked for his father.

The boy found his father sitting with a family who wore polar bear skins. They all sat hunched over a smoothed portion of snow next to the fire's light, gesturing with pointed sticks at the drawings carved into the snow. When the boy called out a greeting and crouched beside them, they looked at him with smiles. His father pointed at the drawing on the ground. It seemed to be some sort of map.

"This family says there is a better place to catch seals

during spring that I have never heard about." His father smiled and turned back to the polar bear–clad family, his face alive with interest.

Piŋa stood and continued walking through the camps, taking his time to greet every guest. He also made sure to ask if there was anything the people needed. One family asked for a tent, as theirs had gotten damaged on the way to the gathering. Piŋa easily found replacement skins so that they had someplace warm to sleep. At one point he found two men arguing at the edge of the camp.

One man had accused the other of stealing some food that they had brought, but of course the other family was adamant that they had not taken anything. After listening to both men and watching as the situation grew heated, Piŋa remembered the lessons he learned in the eagles' home, in particular his interaction with angry Alik and indifferent Pula. The boy did his best to remind the men about the singing and dancing that was to come. He sat with them until the flames of anger dimmed.

It was awkward at first, but he knew how anger could escalate if not addressed, and he couldn't fail the Eagle Mother. The boy assured both families that they would be fed well the next day. He even returned later to speak to the man who believed his food was stolen, bringing him some dried caribou meat to make sure the man and his family felt heard.

At last, Piŋa made his way back to his family's sod house. He would need to prepare the drums for everyone tomorrow. He had noticed that there were a few people he had invited that did not come. Alik and his family were not there, and the tall man and his daughter were also not there. But even then, looking out over the camps, the boy felt happier than he had ever thought possible.

The next day the boy and his family got up early, eager to start the festivities. They opened up two of the storage mounds and emptied their contents. Some of their guests joined to help. Portions were shared with each family: a generous helping of caribou meat, his mother's delicious whipped caribou fat, and a whole salmon. After that bounty was passed out, they made another round to each camp, with some dried meat, frozen masu root, and a ladle of rendered seal fat. Next there was fermented plant pudding, and some dried and smoked lake trout. The boy soon lost track of the many types of food that kept coming, and once every camp got their share, the eating began in earnest. That left one underground storage mound full of food, which they would open when they were celebrating inside the qalgi.

All the campfires were lit, and food was cooking everywhere. The smell was amazing. Some of their guests shared food that they had brought with them, including expertly fermented fish heads, pokes full of berries of every color, dried sheep meat, and dried seaweed, all of which they happily handed out.

One of his most favorite foods was from a large family he had just met. The mother and father had eight children between them. They showed him food that they had made from finding the stash of roots that lemmings hid for the winter. The mix of roots was washed well and then soaked in seal oil. A boy not much younger than himself came forward and gave him a waterproof pouch full of the special treat, his large smile rounding his cheeks. Pinja was not used to receiving gifts from strangers, and he was sure to thank them profusely. But what the boy heard was even better than the food.

The camps were filled with the sounds of laughter and animated conversation. Children giggled and ran around in excited groups. The air hummed with stories. The boy and his family floated from tent to tent, sampling foods they had never tasted before and making sure everyone was taken care of.

When the sun began to set, the families began to make their way to the qalgi, all vying for the best seats. The hall was filled with the buzz of excitement and hushed conversation.

The boy was pleased to see that the qalgi was large enough to fit everyone comfortably and still have a space in the center for dancing. They brought the rest of the food into the hall, and they all ate until they were so full that it was impossible to eat anymore.

An old man wearing a short parka made from marmot skins stood. He whistled loudly, grabbing the attention of those around him, and they quieted, turning toward him to see what he was about. He smiled at the crowd.

"Quyanaq to the family who invited us here," he said. "Our travel was easy at this time of year. We did have an incident, though, on the way here, which involved an especially deep, swift river. Would anyone like to hear how we finally crossed it? With no wood?" A few of the people cheered him on, gathering around him to hear him better.

Another woman stood farther down the hall, gathering her own circle of people as she began telling a story about finding a magic piece of driftwood that made your toes grow minds of their own if you jumped over it, and how she had seen a boy yelling at his own feet to obey him.

A young man down the hall stood and told a rousing story about hunting a polar bear who had an extra set of legs. People young and old moved from space to space and sat down to hear the story that interested them the most. The hall was soon filled with storytelling: some told histories of their family, some told mythical stories about fantastic feats, and others told stories of adventures that just happened to them the last summer. The hall hummed with the cadence and rhythm of words.

When there was a lull in the storytelling, the boy and his family walked to the center of the hall. They picked up the drums, and everyone hushed. The boy and his family began to sing a song of gift-giving that they had created. Others soon stood up. The boy recognized the wolverine-clothed people from his stay in the Eagle Mother's place, but he chose to say nothing when he saw the quiet and small-statured Pula raise her eyebrows. They picked up the other drums and began echoing the words that the boy and his family sang.

When the song settled, his mother rose and started

handing out the gifts and small trinkets that she had made, first raising them above her head to show them off, then placing them in front of the person receiving the gift. She handed out small whales and polar bears carved from ivory and bone, hollow and capped caribou leg bones that were small and sturdy enough to hold delicate needles, beads with polished surfaces, warm mittens, and tiny but deadly ivory fishhooks. Each gift was met with gasps of awe and appreciation. When she was finished, his mother walked back to the drum and picked it up, her face flushed with gratitude at the murmured praise on the quality of her work.

His father rose next and handed out his gifts to the families. He, too, raised them above his head to show the audience—obsidian knives and slate ulus glinting in the dim light; arrowheads carved from chert; coils of rope made from the thick, tough hide of the bearded seal; and giant, glowing tusks of walrus. These gifts were met with excitement and pleasure. His father was reserved, but he walked with more pride, and his eyes glittered with thanks. All the while, the song continued its comforting drone.

The boy's turn was next, and he got up and began handing out the furs that he and his father had dried and tanned. Hands reached out, eager for the gifts, and people sat crooning over the skins, running their fingers through the deep strands of the various pelts, the impossibly white fur of the Arctic fox, the black-tipped gray of the wolf, the deep brown of fall-time caribou, and the bristlier and sun-streaked wolverine furs. They all cheered and laughed at the boy's flushed face, as waves of gratitude engulfed him and his family. When they were finished, the whole room ended the song with a flourish and a yell that made everyone laugh and call out requests for more songs.

It was time. The boy brought out the eagle drum and attached it carefully to the sealskin rope he had hung from the rafters. It was plainer than the one at the eagles' qalgi, but Piŋa knew it would sound the same sweet, vital note.

The crowd hushed and waited expectantly as the boy readied himself. In his mind, he ran through the song that he had prepared especially for this moment. And then, slowly, remembering the sound at mountaintop, he struck the drum, mimicking Eagle Mother's heartbeat.

It echoed, filling the hall with the power that was *her* presence. All other sounds ceased. The boy closed his eyes and circled the drum, striking it in a rhythm that he knew by heart. He raised his voice so that *she* would hear. His voice was clear and strong:

Golden Mother
Fly again
Golden Mother
We sing your gift
Golden Mother
We praise your wisdom

He spread his arms wide and cried out, emulating the sharp calls of an eagle. He heard the people around him gasp, but he was steadfast and continued his song:

Golden Mother
Our heartbeats sing
Golden Mother
Our drums are strong
Golden Mother
We praise your wisdom

He heard his own mother's voice rise clear and strong as she stood up and circled the boy in the opposite direction. She moved gracefully, her knees bent in time with the drums, arms spread wide as she mimicked the great bird she knew from her son's stories. And she sang:

Young boy
Your task is great
Young boy
I see these people
Young boy
I am wise

And it seemed for just an instant that his mother *was* the great golden Eagle Mother herself, as she dipped and then cried out exactly as an eagle would. It sent a shiver down the boy's spine when he watched her sit down again next to his father, her head bowed as if she were suddenly very tired.

With a flourish and a loud boom of the drum, the boy ended his song. For a moment, there was complete silence. Then the men let out loud appreciative yells and the women whooped their approval as they stomped their feet. Piŋa sat down, the echo of the eagle's heart song still beating through his body.

They stayed up for the rest of the night, dancing and singing. Eventually, the rest of the people came forward with songs of their own—songs of hunting and sewing, of strange creatures and mythical places, of fantastic hunting experiences, and simple songs of a mother's love for her children.

Even the boy who had gifted him the bag of roots in seal oil earlier stood up and did a comical dance and a song about a lemming who wanted to fly and so dipped himself in seal oil, and now, the song said, you could find little brown birds on the tundra who sang with high piping voices.

Piŋa marveled at the feelings filling his chest and mind. He felt as if his very soul had grown and found roots in the people around him. He felt more connected than he had ever before, connected to the world, connected to the life around him, and connected to his parents. The celebrations filled him with such inspiration, such wonder, and an enduring strength. He felt his humanity blossom with new insight and a deeper sense of stability. The future held fewer unknowns, and with all this knowledge he felt more deeply accepted . . . flaws and all.

It was a night that rewrote history, some say, and fulfilled a need that no one knew they had.

25

THE END OF THE FEAST

Soon enough, the sun rose into the Arctic sky, and the sound of songs turned into yawns and drooping eyes. Finally exhausted, people started leaving the great qalgi. Whispering words of gratitude toward the tired boy and his family, and with brief hugs and congratulations to one another, they ducked down into the entrance of the hall, slipped into the tunnel, and disappeared, one by one.

The boy was rubbing oil into the drums and carefully storing them away, nodding every once in a while to those who were leaving, when he felt a strong, familiar presence at his back. Smiling without turning around, he spoke, his voice raw from singing. "Did we make you proud, Aana Eagle?" In reply, he heard the familiar sound of feathers rustling, and the scent of mountains filled the space. The change in atmosphere caught his parents' attention, and they turned to see what was the cause, their faces wide with wonder.

When she spoke, her voice was just as he remembered. "Yes, boy, I am grateful, and I do not regret giving you this burden."

Carefully he set down the drum and turned. She was standing with several others. They all wore gleaming parkas of golden eagle feathers. He recognized Savik, who smiled, and Nautchiaq, and her sister Isiġnaq, but the others were strangers to him.

He raised his eyes and met Eagle Mother's pyrite glance. When he saw her, the breath was torn from his body. She was not the old, smelly woman that he remembered from his time in the aerie. Her hair was the color of dried tundra grass, and sparks of fire traced their lengths down to her knees. Her skin was dark and rich and smooth as eggshells; no more did wrinkles mar her face. She stood taller than he remembered, her body straight and young. The parka she wore was clean and bright and shone with a luminescence that outshone those around her. Her eyes, though, were the same—heavy with knowledge and power.

She leaned closer to him. When she saw his surprise, a slight smile appeared on her lips. Her voice left gold sparks in the air, and he could have sworn that she was not just speaking but singing.

"And now you see why we went through so much trouble, boy," she sang. "Atuqtuni, uamittuni suli niqinaqiruni nutaaġuqtitchugait tiŋmiaqpaaluit—singing, dancing, and feasting make old, cranky eagles young! We both need this connection to survive, you for the connections in your soul, and me . . . well, I need it to stay immortal. Connections, boy, our world is nothing but connections." She smiled again and walked past him, leaving him to gape at the empty space where she had stood.

His parents, who were watching all this from a distance, rushed up to him nervously. His mother placed her hand on his arm, squeezing it tight, while his father stood close beside him. He looked at his parents' faces, saw the love that they had for him reflected in their eyes, and he knew that this was not only the end of his trials with the eagles, but the beginning of their life's work. He saw the chance to make the memory of his brothers' lives forever in music and dance, through the teachings of the eagles. And that was more than they could hope for.

Belatedly, the boy and his parents slipped out the entrance to watch their guests leave.

It was then that they saw what was happening. As the guests passed through the opening to the qalgi, they reached up and lifted their hoods. As their hoods fell over their faces, their bodies began to change. They began to rearrange themselves like water; arms and legs shifted, and parkas sank into flesh and became sleek fur or feather. Once transformed, they stretched, and snouts and whiskers nodded at the sky where several huge golden eagles lazily floated above the scene, wings propped up by a warm updraft. Though they had been humans when they spent the night in the qalgi, they were now becoming wolves, wolverines, great snowy owls, and all manner of animals as they made their way into the daylight. The human footprints in the snow were soon replaced by various animal tracks, scattering in all directions. In respectful silence, the boy and his parents watched as the guests trotted or loped or flew off into the distance.

The boy who had gifted Piŋa the bag of tasty roots emerged from the qalgi, wearing a sleek brown parka with a large white ivory medallion on his chest. Before he pulled his hood over his head, he waved at Piŋa and his family, wide cheeks smiling with genuine amusement. When he pulled his hood over his head, he shrank down into a small brown creature with a white patch of fur on his chest. The boy waved back as his lemming friend disappeared quickly into the grass. The last to leave were the two round beavers, still chattering and chuckling in their high-pitched voices.

The boy and his parents watched the sunrise in a daze.

Then, with a quickness that belied her age, his mother turned toward them and crossed her arms. Her gaze shone like obsidian. "We will have to do this again . . . with people, that is. We must start preparing soon. We will need a better way to get word to the other humans. So we'll have to plan that. Maybe we should build another storage underground just in case we need the room. But right now, we have to clean. Don't just stand there! Start cleaning!" And she bustled about, picking up what was left behind by the guests.

The boy and his father sighed and began helping her.

It took them days to clean up, but as they cleaned, they also talked about the next great feast and planned on making trips together to find the other Iñupiat and to show them what Eagle Mother had gifted them. It was a beginning, one that would ensure that the Iñupiaq people would never again be alone. And that those old eagles would stay forever young.

AUTHOR'S NOTE

This story of the origins of the Messenger Feast was passed down orally from generation to generation for hundreds, perhaps thousands, of years among the Iñupiat of the Arctic Circle. After the encroachment of the missionaries into Indigenous territories and communities, stories like these were essentially banned because of their association with Inuit culture. Iñupiaq songs and dances were also banned, and this story and many like it shrank and became nothing but brief whispers shared in passing. As our people fought for our rights to practice our culture and won those rights back, and as acceptance of our heritage and history became important to the health and well-being of our population, the festival was resurrected.

We relied on the Elders' accounts of it from when they were children, as well as photos and oral histories. These small, precious recollections had survived famine, disease, damnation by religion, and the encroaching high-tech society. The first modern festival based on this feast was convened sometime after I had left to go to college out of state. When I attended it for the first time, I became curious about the festival's origin story.

I remember that day, sitting so close to other people on the hard, unforgiving wood of the gym bleachers. I had only moved back to northern Alaska the year before to start teaching and was easily intimidated at only twenty-four years old. I didn't have a whole lot of friends, and even though I was surrounded by relatives, I was still getting to know them. I thought getting out and doing more community and cultural events would help me connect faster. I waved and nodded and smiled in the direction of people who yelled my name to say hi. The air was stagnant and filled with the smell of tanned hides and sweating bodies. The murmuring voices around me were frequently sliced by quick bursts of laughter that would fade into embarrassed giggles. Hundreds of people flowed around the building like anxious worms, trying to wiggle into a spot that would give them a better view of the dancers in the center of the gym floor. With slow, stealthy movements, I grabbed my coat and tugged on it a little, trying to slip it from underneath the old woman sitting next to me. Unfortunately—or maybe fortunately—she noticed.

"Do you know why the men run at the beginning of the feast, Panik?" she said.

My face warmed as she used the familiar word for daughter. I tried to smile and carefully avoid her glance. "Naakka. No, Aana," I replied. I could smell her now, the smell all old people have, something dry and dusty, like the years that separate us.

"They used to go and run for miles to find other Iñupiat, because back in the day, we were separated and didn't like each other. We were all alone before that boy got kidnapped. Do you know the story, Panik?"

A story, I thought, and my heart sparked. I love old stories, collect them like I collect beach glass. Slowly, I met her gaze and shook my head no.

Wisps of fine silver hair floated above her head haphazardly. She wore a fur parka complete with wolf ruff. I wondered why she wasn't sweating. And then she began to speak. Her voice was soothing, and her words were clipped and wrought with a tongue more used to speaking a different language. I could not help it; I closed my eyes and listened. She told me this story of the boy kidnapped by eagles.

It is an amazing thing to attend this feast and festival. All cares are washed away by the sound of joyous, heartrending music. After perhaps hundreds of years, it has gained a name: Kivgiġñiq, the Messenger Feast, named for the epic journey special runners were given to make. Talented and robust young people who were known to have great memories were given sticks and told to "find the others and bring them here." They ran for hundreds of miles, recording who would be coming and what foods they would bring by tying "reminders" on a stick.

When it was time, numerous Iñupiat across the Arctic Slope would steadily make their way to the appointed time and place, bringing with them what they could to share and trade with others. It was a feast held only in times of abundance, and to this day it is considered a great honor to attend.

Much has changed since the boy was taken to the eagles' nest. Instead of making their arduous treks by sled, boat, or foot, many take airplanes to shorten the journey. The mayor of Utqiagvik announces the date of the celebration via email and Facebook posts, and there is no need for a messenger anymore. Stores of raw meat and supplies once buried beneath the tundra for preservation are joined now by more modern foods and delicacies in shiny sterile refrigerators. Historically, a stuffed golden eagle was hung from one of the rafters to represent the Eagle Mother's presence, but of course, since it is a protected species, this has not been done for years. At one point, the people of Barrow convinced a museum to let them borrow an eagle. I often wish I'd been there to see the great eagle, encased in its glass box, presiding over the feast, silently watching over the dancers.

Much has remained unchanged, though. People still travel great distances to become reacquainted with family and friends, to introduce new songs and dances, and to share in the bounty of good years. They still hang the rectangular hollow box from the rafters and sing special songs, the men wearing winged headdresses and shouting with joy, the women dancing with arms spread and heads bowed demurely. The dancers come from every village—some even from different countries—to celebrate and fill the space with dancing and songs meant to entertain, inspire, or leave you in wonder. The Inuit people inhabit most of the Arctic

Circle across the globe, including countries such as the U.S., Canada, Greenland, and Russia, and they attend whenever they can. Gifts are exchanged, to the delight and laughter of everyone present, and mounds of food are shared.

I am never ashamed to admit that hearing my people sing and dance brings sorrowful tears to my eyes and an ache to my heart. It is celebrating a part of me, my culture, that is not seen or celebrated very often. It is saying, "Look! Look how beautiful this part of you is!" And it is, in a sense, about how we are listening to our ancestors calling to us through the distance of years. Those connections still hold true.

Often on boating and hunting trips into the mountains, I spot a golden eagle flying on wings tinged with copper, and it makes me wonder if that old woman is still alive, watching us, getting younger with each of our gatherings. But the greatest and most important reason for the gathering is still with us—to bring the Iñupiaq people together in peace and celebration, to unite us as one.

ACKNOWLEDGMENTS

First and foremost, I would like to thank Dr. Pausauraq Jana Harcharek, as this book would not have existed without her belief in and encouragement of my abilities, and her multi-faceted support over the many years this book was developed. Her dedication and love of our culture and people are inspiring, always. Thanks also to Debby Dahl Edwardson for making opportunities available for me to realize my dream of writing, and for making that first step much less scary than it could have been. And an especially loud thanks to my husband for his patience as I learned a new craft, and for his support as I stepped into unknown territory. Thank you to my daughter Taktuk, for standing at my desk and telling me my artwork was good when I needed it the most, and thank you to my daughter Kanaaq, for the best baby hugs that erased so much of my self-doubt.

Special thanks also go to my editor, Connie Hsu, for her exquisite vision and gentle hand. I am so grateful to have been able to learn from her. I could not have asked for a better experience for my debut book. Thank you to Aurora Parlagreco for your talent as an art director; the art in this book is all the more beautiful for it. And thank you to Nicolás Ore-Giron and Mekisha Telfer for your insight in the honing of the manuscript.

Thanks also go to my agent, Faye Bender, whose understanding of my vision and goals has helped me become more confident in so many ways.

Thank you to every single cousin, uncle, aunt, grandparent, teacher, friend, and passing acquaintance that told me their stories and stories that have been passed down for generations. These stories are so *good* that they molded me into a storyteller. There is so much Iñupiaq wealth contained in those words, and they are all the more valuable for surviving our people's trials and tribulations.

And last but not least, thank you to all of the Iñupiaq

children who have inspired me to reach for every opportunity; you are our greatest treasure, our greatest pride, and in you we see such brilliant hope. Never believe anything less.